Finding Buck McHenry

Finding Buck McHenry

by Alfred Slote

SCHOLASTIC INC.
New York Toronto London Auckland Sydney

ISBN 0-590-46165-6

Copyright © 1991 by Alfred Slote. All rights reserved. Published by Scholastic Inc., 730 Broadway, New York, NY 10003, by arrangement with HarperCollins Children's Books, a division of HarperCollins Publishers.

12 11 10 9 8 7 6 5 4 3 2 1   3 4 5 6 7 8/9

Printed in the U.S.A.   40

First Scholastic printing, March 1993

For Jim Shaw
scholar, source, second baseman

Finding
Buck
McHenry

1

Dad says it's wrong to make up scenarios for real life. (As though I did it on purpose.) He says real life has a way of telling you off.

He's talking about Mr. Henry, of course.

Mr. Henry is the custodian where I used to go to school. My name is Jason Ross. I'm eleven years old and I live in Arborville, Michigan.

There's no reason you should have heard of me. But there was, I thought, every reason you should have heard of Mr. Henry. Not under that name, of course. But under his real name—Buck McHenry.

I'm jumping the gun now. Dad says that if I insist on telling this story, "which doesn't do you a lot of credit, Jason," he adds, I ought at least to start at the beginning.

The beginning was when I got kicked off the Baer Machine baseball team. And that happened during our last intrasquad practice game of the spring. I was the batter and I'd just hit a hard ground ball down the third-base line.

"Run, Jason, run!" the guys on my side yelled. (We'd divided the team in half for this practice game.)

I ran hard. If I beat out the ball for a hit, Greg Conklin would score from third and we'd tie them and go into extra innings. I knew I could beat it out too, because as I took off for first, I watched Art Silver, our third baseman, back up on my ball. Ahead of me I saw Tim Corrigan, our first baseman, stretching to receive Art's throw. It would be close but I could make it, I thought. I lunged for the bag and hit it with my right toe just before, I thought, the ball arrived.

"Out," Mr. Borker called. He's our coach and was umping from behind the pitcher.

"Out?" I couldn't believe it.

"Yes, out, Jason. When you should've been safe. For Pete's sake, when you run that slowly to first, are you thinking about something?"

"Jason's thinking about baseball cards, Coach," Pete Diaz, our center fielder, said running by us to the bench.

"Jason's always thinking about baseball cards," Greg Conklin laughed.

Kevin Kovich chimed in, "Jason was thinkin'

that soon as practice was over he was goin' down to The Grandstand and buy more cards."

"Okay, guys," I said, getting down on the bench with them. "Take it easy, huh?"

I try not to let their taunting get to me. Some athletes collect cards; others don't. I'm one who does. Baseball cards are an important part of my life.

Mr. Borker shook his head. "Ballplayers don't think about baseball cards while they're playing, Jason."

I wanted to tell him that I wasn't thinking about baseball cards. I wasn't thinking about anything except beating Art's throw to first. But I had the sense to keep my mouth shut. You never get anywhere arguing with a coach. In any sport. Coaches are always right. Even when they're wrong.

"Daydream while you're playing ball, Jason," Mr. Borker went on, "and you'll never win a game for your team."

That stopped me. Not the daydream part but the way he said, win a game for *your* team, as if my team wasn't Baer Machine. As if Baer Machine wasn't *our* team. I guess I should have sensed then what was coming. But I didn't.

"All right, everyone down on the bench and let's have some quiet," Mr. Borker said, even though he was the only one talking.

He looked at his clipboard. "Next Wednesday we've got our first real practice game. Against the Bank team. Who *cannot* make it?"

No one raised their hand. He looked at me. "I'll be there," I said, wondering why he was singling me out. Did he *not* want me to be there? I was the backup catcher. If Tug Murphy ever got hurt, I'd be taking his place. Of course, I'd get into the game anyway. By league regulations, everyone has to play at least one inning. If we're way ahead, Mr. Borker lets me catch the last inning. If it's tight, he sticks me in right field.

"We'll all be there, Coach," Tug said. "This year we're gonna get those Bank guys."

"We shoulda got 'em last year," Tim Corrigan said.

"That's right," Mr. Borker said. "We should've taken them last year. But this year we will. We've got the pitching, the hitting, and the depth." His eyes roamed from one player to another. "Maybe too much depth," he added, and once again those eyes settled on me.

And still I didn't think anything of it. I was wondering how a team could have too much depth. In the major leagues depth helps a team overcome injuries. You don't have too many injuries in Little League. But what you do have are kids going on vacations. Vacations are Little League injuries. So even in Little League you need extra bodies.

"We've got fourteen players," Mr. Borker said. "A team in the eleven-year-old league shouldn't carry more than thirteen. Most of the other teams have extra players too. Last night we had a coaches' meeting and Chuck Axelrod, our new league president, said—"

"Chuck Axelrod, the sportscaster?" Art Silver interrupted.

I was glad Art had the nerve to ask. I think we were all wondering that. Chuck Axelrod was Channel 4's top sportscaster. His Saturday night *Sportsline* show was the most popular sports show on TV. None of us could believe someone as famous as Chuck Axelrod would live here in Arborville.

"That's right, Art," Mr. Borker said. He seemed annoyed at the idea of Chuck Axelrod living here in Arborville and being involved with our league. "We're supposed to be honored to have Chuck Axelrod become our league director."

"I didn't know he lived in Arborville, Coach," Kovich said.

"He moved here about a month ago and some

7

genius in the Recreation Department got the idea we could get a lot of publicity for the Arborville kids' baseball program if we asked him to be director of one of the leagues. Since he's got an eleven-year-old kid he wants to get on a team, they asked him to direct our league. Right away Axelrod decided there were enough extra players and brand-new players like his own kid to form a new team. To make a long story short, Baer Machine has agreed to contribute one player to the new team."

He said "Baer Machine" as though it was one of his toolmaking machines that had made the decision. Mr. Borker was part owner of the Baer Machine Company and *he'd* made the decision. I wondered who he was going to cut. I looked around. None of the other guys were looking around. They were all studying their mitts or their shoes as though they'd never seen them before.

And then it hit me. No, I thought, he wouldn't do that. He wouldn't cut me. I'm not the worst player on the team. I'm not the best but I'm not the worst. And suppose Tug gets hurt? Who would catch then?

I looked at Mr. Borker, hoping by now he was eyeing someone else. But he was still looking at me. My heart began to pound. My face felt hot. I knew it had turned red.

"Jason, this is as hard for me as it is for you."

His words hung in the air in front of me. I wished I was a million miles away and couldn't hear them.

"But catcher is your position, Jason, and you'll be a starter for the new team."

I didn't want to be a starting catcher for a new team. I liked being Tug's backup. He was the best catcher in the league. It was no disgrace being his backup. Besides, this was the only team I'd ever played with.

"It could be a great opportunity for you, Jason."

I felt my eyes getting moist. I gritted my teeth. Whatever you do, I told myself, don't cry!

"What's the name of Jason's new team?" Greg Conklin asked quietly. I think he felt bad for me.

"The team hasn't been formed yet, Greg. It will be getting a new sponsor and a new coach."

"It'll be like an expansion team, won't it, Coach?" Tug asked. He was trying to make me feel better too. Tears sprang into my eyes. I cry when people are nice to me more than when they're mean.

"That's right, Tug, that's just what it'll be like. A major-league expansion team. Lots of good ballplayers got their start on expansion teams, Jason."

He didn't have to tell me that. I had an Ace Bubble Gum Expansion Player set. It included people like Bill Stoneman (Ace 550), who pitched two no-hitters after he'd been let go, and Dean Chance (Golden Ace 215), who became a Cy Young winner with his new team.

I could feel everyone looking at me now. I took a deep breath. "What do I do now, Mr. Borker?" I asked.

He looked relieved. "You just sit tight, Jason. I'll turn your name in to Chuck Axelrod soon as I get home. He'll be in touch with you and with all the other expansion players. And the new players."

That meant all over town kids were being cut this morning. I wasn't alone. That made me feel a little better.

Mr. Borker went back to his clipboard. "All right, let's move on. Wednesday we play the Bank right here at Eberwoods at five o'clock. I'll pitch Cal for the first two innings and then bring in Tim and—"

He looked up and his eyes fell on me again.

I could see him wishing I was gone already. (Even though he'd just told me to sit tight.)

"Jason, how'd you like to do me a big favor?"

He's figured out a way to get rid of me, I thought.

"Those bases out there, I borrowed them from the school. Mr. Henry, the custodian, is up there. There's an adult-league basketball game going on and he has to keep the school open. How'd you like to return the bases to him?"

I didn't want to return the bases for him. I didn't want to do him any favors. But what choice did I have? I was off the team. I might as well be gone.

"Okay," I said, and stood up.

"Thanks, Jason. And listen"—his face took on a phony sincere look—"I know everyone joins me in wishing you good luck with your new team."

"Yeah, good luck, Jayce," someone said.

And the others mumbled, "Yeah, good luck, Jayce. Take it easy, Jason. We'll see ya around. Yeah, see ya, Jason. See ya, see ya, see ya . . ."

And that's how it goes when you get cut from the only team you've ever played with. That's how you say good-bye to guys you've known since kindergarten.

It's "See ya, Jason, see ya, man, see ya, see ya, see ya."

I looked at them. "Yeah," I said. "See ya."

I ran out on the field to get the bases. I ran hard. I didn't look back.

2

Two years ago when I was in third grade, my family moved across town. I don't go to Eberwoods School anymore, but I remembered Mr. Henry, the custodian there, real well. He was a tall, gray-haired old man who always had a friendly word for everyone as he pushed his broom down the hall. He knew every kid's name, too.

I doubted he'd remember me now, though.

Mr. Henry was sitting by the back door of the school. The school's up a slight hill past center field. It was like center-field bleachers in Tiger Stadium. If Mr. Henry had been out there awhile, he probably had seen our intrasquad game.

"Hi, Mr. Henry," I said. "I got some bases for you."

"I see that, boy." He got up. "And I thank you for bringing 'em up here."

"That's okay."

He peered down at me. "Say, aren't you the one made that last out?"

I felt my face turn red all over again. This just wasn't my day. "Yes, sir."

He laughed. "Well, you sure run a lot harder picking up those bases than you run to first."

"Did *you* think I was out, Mr. Henry?"

"You were out by four feet. Four big feet. You stayed in that batter's box so long I thought the train was going to leave without you."

I laughed. It was funny how he put it. It didn't hurt. "I guess maybe I *was* out."

"You were out all right. But you got the right attitude, bouncing back like you did, running hard to pick up bases. I always said you can't keep a good man down. All right, you can give me those bases now and head on back to your team."

I looked back at the diamond. They were still there. I'd have to go back for my bike and glove. Better to hang out here till they were gone. I didn't want any more "see ya's."

"I can take the bases into the gym for you, Mr. Henry."

"That's nice of you, son. But your coach is going to be mad at you if you don't get back right away. I'll take them from you."

14

I held on tight to the bases. "He's not my coach anymore." I tried to sound cheerful about it. "He just cut me from the team. I don't want to go back there till they're gone."

Mr. Henry's lips pursed in a surprised silent whistle. "He cut you?"

"Yes, sir."

"For not beating out that ground ball?"

"I guess so."

His tongue made "tsk, tsk" sounds against his front teeth. "Well, that's how it goes sometimes. Sometimes they cut the best along with the worst."

"Thanks, but I'm not the best."

"You aren't the worst either." He held the back door open for me. "I've seen lots better ballplayers than you cut from ball clubs." I marched into the school with my arms full of bases. I could hear the sounds of the adult basketball game coming from the gym.

"You ever hear of Willie Mays, boy?"

"Ace 675," I said.

"What's that?"

"That's the number of my 1955 Mays baseball card. It's a pretty valuable card. It's not worth near as much as a 1952 Mickey Mantle, but it's worth a lot."

"How come?"

15

"How come what?"

"How come Willie Mays isn't worth as much as Mickey Mantle?"

"I don't know." Nobody'd ever asked me that before. It wasn't the kind of thing you ever thought about. It was enough to know the prices of baseball cards. They were always changing.

"Willie Mays was a greater player, wasn't he? They played the same position in the same years, didn't they? Willie Mays had better numbers, didn't he?" Mr. Henry was challenging me. I wondered what he was so upset about.

"I think Mays did have better stats than Mantle."

"Well, if Willie Mays had better numbers than Mickey Mantle and he was a better ballplayer, how come his card's worth less?"

"I don't know."

"You ought to find out. You've got to think about those things, young man. You've got to ask yourself how come things are the way they are."

Jim Davis, who owned The Grandstand, would know, I thought. I'd stop there on the way home and ask him.

"Willie Mays was the greatest center fielder who ever lived," Mr. Henry said emphatically.

"If he was so great, Mr. Henry, how come he got cut?"

Mr. Henry blinked. Then he laughed. "You come back with a good pitch, boy."

"Well, you said he got cut."

"He did get cut. And they were right to cut him."

"Who cut him?"

"The New York Giants when he first came into the major leagues. Willie was strikin' out all the time. He was too anxious to show the New York folks that he'd be as good up there as he'd been with the Birmingham Black Barons."

"The Birmingham who?"

"The Birmingham Black Barons. Willie played center field for them when he was sixteen." Mr. Henry's voice turned soft as he began to remember. "Willie Mays was a boy among men way back then, but you could see the greatness in him already. He could run like a deer, hit like a mule, and throw you out from deep center field. He could do it all. It was there from the beginning. I saw it with my own eyes."

I stared at Mr. Henry. He'd seen Willie Mays play when he was sixteen?

"Willie Mays was put on earth to play baseball.

17

Not football. Not basketball. Just baseball. It was in his chromosomes. You know what chromosomes are, boy?"

"They're what makes us look like our parents."

"That's right. Well, Willie Mays had chromosomes for baseball."

"Wow."

"The Black Barons were good. But when he played for them, Willie made them great."

"I never heard of them."

"That right?" He didn't seem surprised. "You probably never heard of the Kansas City Monarchs neither."

"No, sir."

"Or the Homestead Grays?"

I shook my head.

"Or the best of them all. The Pittsburgh Crawfords?"

Was he making these teams up? I went on shaking my head.

"Josh Gibson caught for the Crawfords. Now I suspect you may have heard of Josh Gibson."

I was really embarrassed. "No, sir." This was kind of awful. I had over two thousand baseball cards and there wasn't a Josh Gibson on any of them. Nor a Crawford nor a Homestead Gray.

"Josh Gibson was only the greatest hitter who ever lived. That's all he was."

18

"Was he a better hitter than Willie Mays, Mr. Henry?"

"Yes, he was. He was better than Hank Aaron. Better than Mickey Mantle, Ted Williams. Better than Pete Rose, George Brett, Wade Boggs, your Cansecos and Strawberries. Better than any of your players today. You name 'em and Josh was better than. Better than Ty Cobb and Babe Ruth. Why, I saw Josh hit a home run out of Yankee Stadium. Up and over and out of it. Now Babe Ruth, great as he was, and I'm not denying his greatness, Babe Ruth never did that."

Mr. Henry looked at me under my load of bases. They were getting heavy. I was hoping he'd offer to take them again. But he didn't.

"I expect you *have* heard of Satchel Paige?"

Finally I'd heard of someone beside Willie Mays. "Sure. He pitched for the Cleveland Indians." I had a 1949 Satchel Paige (Ace 129).

"Well, before Satchel pitched in the so-called big leagues, he pitched for the Pittsburgh Crawfords. And Josh Gibson was his catcher. What a pair they were. Old Josh in his rocking-chair squat and Paige firing those bullets. I tell you another great one was on the Crawfords those years. Cool Papa Bell. You hear of him?"

Here we go again, I thought. "No, sir," I said.

"Fastest man ever to play the game. Cool Papa was so fast, he'd often get hit by his own line drives."

I laughed. Mr. Henry stopped walking. He stopped so suddenly, I bumped into him with the bases. We were smack in the middle of the school where the two main corridors intersected.

"What's your name, boy?"

"Jason Ross."

"You don't look familiar. You go to school here?"

"I used to. We moved when I was in third grade. I go to Sampson Park School now."

"That's okay. It doesn't matter where you go so long as you go. Now, Jason Ross, you set those bases down."

"Here?"

"That's right. Right there on the floor."

I didn't hesitate. I set down the bases on the floor. And rubbed my arms and wrists to get the circulation back.

Mr. Henry didn't notice. He had taken a key from his big key ring attached to his belt and was unlocking a closet door that said on the front: MACK HENRY, CUSTODIAN.

"You know why you run so slow to first, Jason Ross?"

"No, sir."

"You stood there at the plate looking at where you hit the ball."

The second he said that, I knew that was just what I'd done. I'd stood there watching Art back up on my ground ball.

"Nobody in this world can run and look at the same time."

He rummaged around in the closet and came out with a long push broom.

Had I brought dirt in with my spikes? I didn't see any. Though I probably shouldn't be wearing baseball shoes inside the school. They could ruin the wax on the floors. Luckily, Mr. Henry hadn't spotted my shoes.

"You can see without looking. You've *got* to see without looking."

He unscrewed the stick from the broom and tossed it at me.

I caught it. It would have bopped me on the nose if I hadn't.

"I'm going to prove that to you, Jason Ross. That's your bat."

He picked up two of the bases, leaving one near me. He marched down the hall with the other two and dropped one of them at his feet.

"All right, Jason Ross," he called down the

hall to me, "step up to the plate."

I didn't move. I wanted to know what he was going to do first.

"C'mon, boy. I haven't got all day. That's home plate there. You just step up to it."

He was standing about sixty feet from me.

"Jason, you are trying my patience. Get in there."

Still I didn't move. I don't like to do things unless I know why I'm doing them.

"Jason," he said softly, "this lesson isn't going to hurt you any. It might even do you some good. Now get up there and get your bat back."

What kind of lesson was he talking about? Well, there was only one way to find out. I stepped up to the plate. At least no one was watching.

"Good. Now get your front elbow up a bit. That's it. Now, boy, as soon as this imaginary ball arrives, you are going to hit an imaginary ground ball down that other corridor. That's where third base is. But you are not going to look once at where you hit the ball. You can see out of the corner of your eye where your ball went. You can see without turning your head to look. You are just going to run like the wind to this base, which is first base. You are going to run, Jason Ross, like there were hot coals under your feet. You understand me?"

"Yes, sir."

"Get set now. I'm throwing smoke."

And then right there in the middle of Eberwoods School, old, gray-haired Mr. Henry, the school custodian, went into a full windup.

And as he did, something strange happened. He didn't look so old. He looked tall and young and powerful as he kicked high and came down over his head with a smooth motion and fired the imaginary ball.

I swung.

"Run!" he yelled.

I ran. I didn't look down the other corridor where the imaginary ball went. I lifted my feet and ran hard and hit first base with my left shoe. The base slid far down the smooth, waxed floor.

Mr. Henry laughed and slapped me on the back. "Now, if you'd moved like that when you hit that ground ball, you'd still be on your team. You run like that and you'll be getting your share of hits and then some."

He walked back to home plate. "You know who you remind me of, son?"

I shook my head.

"Roy Campanella. You ever hear of him?"

"Sure. He played with the Brooklyn Dodgers.

I've got two Ace Campanella cards."

"Well, before that, my friend, he played with the Baltimore Elite Giants and some other clubs. Just like Jackie Robinson—you've surely heard of him—played with the Monarchs before he was signed by Mr. Branch Rickey and sent to Montreal. Campy now, he was chubby like you. And he was a catcher too. And he could beat out ground balls!"

"How'd you know I was a catcher, Mr. Henry?"

"I've seen you catching."

"Well, I don't catch very much. I don't play very much."

"You will if you hit. If you hit, they've got to play you. Now you go back and tell that coach of yours to give you another chance."

Mr. Henry screwed the stick back into the broom and leaned it against the shelves of cleaning powder, wax, shelves of paper towels, toilet paper, soaps. Then he shut and locked the door that said MACK HENRY, CUSTODIAN on it. He picked up home plate.

"He won't give me another chance, Mr. Henry. I'm gonna be on a new team."

"Well then you're just going to have to come back with your new team and beat that man's socks off. Speaking of which, boy, before you

24

take another step, you take those spikes off. You're wrecking my floor."

And with that he went off toward the gym carrying the bases as though they weighed nothing.

I had to laugh. He'd just proved that you could see without looking. I walked out of the school in my socks. The team meeting was over. The diamond was empty. I sat down on the grass and put my shoes back on. Then I raced over to my bike and glove. I wanted to get down to The Grandstand as fast as possible and check on those players and teams he'd mentioned. If they were real—those Crawfords and Monarchs and Black Barons and Cool Papa Bells and Josh Gibsons—then there'd be baseball cards for them.

Jim Davis down at The Grandstand was always saying, "Truth's in the cards." I believed that. I hurried down there.

3

Southeastern Michigan, where I live, is a hotbed
of baseball card collecting. There are lots of baseball card stores around. But The Grandstand
is the best of them. And that's mostly because
of Jim Davis, who has a great way with kids
and also because he has a lot of great stuff in
the store.

As you enter The Grandstand, the first thing
you see are packs of new Ace bubble gum cards.
They sell for fifty cents each. You get one stick
of gum and fifteen cards. The gum is terrible
but no one buys Ace bubble gum baseball cards
for the gum.

Just past the new cards is a table of old cards.
There are three long boxes there. One box is
marked 5 CENTS EACH, another 10 CENTS
EACH, another 25 CENTS EACH. There are
about two hundred cards in each box. Unless

Jim changes them often, I know what's in those boxes by heart.

After buying a pack or two of new cards, most kids will make a beeline here hoping to find their favorite player for a nickel. This is Detroit Tiger country, so kids are always hoping to come up with a rookie all-star Matt Nokes or an oldie like a 1968 Al Kaline as though Jim would be careless enough to put either a 1968 Kaline or a rookie Nokes or a Cecil Fielder in the nickel, dime, and quarter boxes.

Around this table a lot of trading also takes place. Jim Davis doesn't mind kids trading but he won't let adults trade. He says there are adults who come to the store not to buy but to use it as a trading post.

"No way," says Jim. "I'm paying the rent here."

After you get past the new cards and the old cards there's lots of wonderful things in The Grandstand. There are T-shirts—Detroit Tigers, Lions, Pistons, Red Wings. There are Tigers window insignia, key rings, bumper stickers, wristbands, decals, buttons, baseball caps, backboards for wastepaper baskets, big posters of all different superstars like Wayne Gretzky, Mark McGwire, Ozzie Smith, Magic Johnson, Isiah Thomas, Joe Dumars, Dennis Rodman.

There are warm-up jackets, American League baseballs, old football and baseball programs.

There are books and magazines about every sport imaginable.

Near the cash register are the glass cases with some valuable baseball card sets: traded sets, complete sets, team sets, rookie sets, theme sets like sluggers versus pitchers, record breakers, superstars. Decade Greats—Sportsflicks puts them out.

On the wall behind the glass cases are autographed bats. Jim has a Cecil Fielder bat for fifty bucks. He has a regular Alan Trammel bat for $79.95 and an autographed one for one hundred bucks.

He also has an empty Wheaties box autographed by Pete Rose. Rose's picture is on the box.

"How'd you get the autograph?" I asked Jim once.

"Baseball card show in Dearborn. It cost me eight dollars to get in. So I'm making fifteen dollars on the deal."

"If you sell it."

Jim laughed. "Oh, I'll sell it, Jason."

I wasn't so sure about that. I didn't have twenty-five dollars, but if I did I wouldn't spend it for Pete Rose's name and picture on a Wheaties box. Jim's probably gonna have to go down to Cincinnati to sell it.

Around the other side of the wall is a room with a coffeepot, a small round table, and some chairs. Jim does his private dealing back there.

That Saturday when I went into The Grandstand, it was packed with little kids and their fathers. Jim was behind the counter kidding with people, watching, but never pressuring anyone to buy. He's a collector himself and knows how to talk to kids.

He spotted me right away. "Jason, how's the Baer Machine team doing?"

I still had my Baer Machine baseball shirt on.

"Okay. But I'm not on it anymore. Jim, I want to ask you something."

"What do you mean, you're not on it anymore?"

"I got cut."

"You're kidding?"

"No."

"You've been on that team for years. What'd they cut you for?"

I shrugged. "Not beating out a ground ball."

"That's it?"

"Also, Mr. Borker never liked me. He thinks I think about baseball cards too much." I grinned as I said that. I kind of like teasing Jim a little.

"Does he? Well, I don't think I like *him*. As far as I'm concerned, you can never think about baseball cards too much." We both laughed. "What are you gonna do now, Jason? Try to hook up with another team?"

"I don't know. Mr. Borker says there's going to be an expansion team in the eleven-year-old league. I may play on it. What I came here about, Jim, is to ask you if you've ever heard of the Birming—"

"Wait a second, Jason. You say there's going to be an expansion team in your league? A new team?"

Jim leaned over the counter. He suddenly had a very interested look on his face.

"Yeah, there's going to be a new team."

"Do they have a sponsor for it yet?"

"I don't know. Why?"

Two little kids had come up behind me to buy some stuff. They could have been on another planet as far as Jim was concerned.

"I've been thinking for some time that The Grandstand ought to sponsor a kids' baseball team."

I almost jumped at the idea but I restrained myself. "We'd be a lousy team, Jim. We'd all be rejects from other teams. We'd give The Grandstand a bad name."

"C'mon, Jason, get a good coach, a couple of key players, and we'll be great." Jim grinned at me. "And every time we win, Jason, instead of going for Dairy Queens, I'll treat you kids to a pack of Ace bubble gum cards. How does that hit you?"

I laughed. "That's a pretty good deal if we win any. Would you coach us, Jim? You could be an owner-manager like Connie Mack (Ace Old Timers 212). He was the last owner-manager, wasn't he?"

"I wouldn't mind being another Connie Mack, Jason. But Connie Mack didn't have a baseball-card store to look after. No, we'll have to find a coach. Someone's father."

"Excuse me," a little voice said from behind me. "Could we buy these cards?"

Two little six-year-olds stood there clutching new packs of Ace gum.

"You sure can. Sorry I didn't see you there. Stick around, Jason. What've you got there, gentlemen?"

"Bubble gum cards."

"I hope you got some good ones."

"We do too, don't we, Mikey?"

"Yeah," Mikey said.

The kids paid for their cards with pennies, nickels, and dimes the way I used to when I was their age. I started to step back up to the counter when a teenage girl slipped in ahead of me. She was holding a poster of Isiah Thomas, the Pistons' great guard.

"How much?" she asked shyly.

"Seven fifty," Jim said.

"That much?"

"You think he's good?"

"I love his smile."

Jim laughed. "All right, for Isiah's smile I'll shave twenty-five cents off the price. Seven twenty-five. That's as low as I can go."

"I'll buy it," the girl said.

"Hey, Jim," I said, "I like the way Mickey Mantle smiles on his 1952 Ace card. Would you let me have it for seven twenty-five?"

That Ace 1952 Mickey Mantle (which I'd been telling Mr. Henry about) fetched two thousand five hundred dollars. Jim didn't own it, of course. But it reminded me of the other thing I had to ask Jim about, even though I still hadn't even asked him about the Birmingham Black Barons and Josh Gibson and Cool Papa Bell. I waited till the girl and her Isiah Thomas poster left.

"Jim, I got a couple of things to ask you about. First, do you think Willie Mays was a better ballplayer than Mickey Mantle?"

"Jason, let's talk about our new team first."

"Just tell me," I begged. "Mantle or Mays. Who was better?"

"Okay. Most people think Mays was the greater ballplayer. Mantle was a superstar too. But most of the time he could only really beat you with his bat. He was a great offensive player. Mays could beat you every which way. Arm, legs, bat, glove. Mantle was injury prone too. Mays had a longer career. Now can we go back to this expansion team?"

"If Mays is considered better, how come Mantle's cards are always worth more?" I was asking Mr. Henry's question.

"It's the market."

"What's that mean?"

"It just means there's a greater demand for Mantle's cards than for Mays's. And it's demand that sends up the price."

"How come there's more demand for Mantle if Mays had the better stats?" Mr. Henry would have asked that.

Jim shrugged. "Who knows? Maybe it's because kids who collect cards are mostly white. I don't know. I just sell cards. I don't analyze them. Now who do I call about sponsoring the expansion team?"

I thought about what Jim just said. It was true you didn't see many black kids collecting, but there had to be some. But even if that was the reason, it was the wrong kind of reason for one card to be worth more than another. It was dumb.

"Jason, I just asked you a question. Who do I call about sponsoring the new team?"

"Huh? Oh. Chuck Axelrod."

"The sportscaster?"

"Yeah."

"Are you kidding me, Jason?"

"No. Mr. Borker says Chuck Axelrod just moved to Arborville and they asked him to direct the eleven-year-old league to get publicity. Mr. Borker says he took it cause he's got a son who's eleven years old and wants to get on a team."

Jim whistled. I could see the wheels turning inside his head. "I like it, Jason. The possibilities are tremendous. Chuck Axelrod living in Arborville, directing the eleven-year-old league, The Grandstand sponsoring a team in his league, his son is on the team, and he gets interested in doing a feature story on The Grandstand for his Saturday *Sportsline* show. How does it grab you, Jason?"

I laughed. "Sounds good."

He opened up the Arborville phone book and started looking through it.

"Now what're you doing?" I said.

"Lookin' up Chuck Axelrod's phone number."

"Can I ask you something else while you do that?"

"You can ask me anything, Jason. But will I have the answer? That's the question. Axelrod, Axelrod. Axel—"

"Did you ever hear of a team called the Birmingham Black Barons?"

"That was a team in the old Negro leagues. Here we are. . . . Axelrod."

"The old Negro leagues?"

"Yeah, those leagues were in operation from about 1900 to 1946, when Jackie Robinson broke the color barrier. There were some great teams too. . . . Axelrod, Alan and Susan; Axelrod, Barry; Axelrod, Bernard . . ."

"Like the Pittsburgh Crawfords?"

"Yeah. And the Homestead Grays and the Kansas City Monarchs and the Detroit Wolves and the Chicago American Giants and the Newark Eagles and . . . and there's no Axelrod, Chuck or Charles. It goes from Bernard to Lawrence."

"Are there baseball cards for those old teams?"

"It's probably a new number. What did you say?"

"Are there baseball cards for those teams?"

"What teams?"

"Jim, for Pete's sake, the teams in the old Negro leagues."

"Andy Armstrong has just put out a collection he put together himself. Here . . . I haven't had a chance to look at them yet."

With one hand Jim dug under the counter and brought up a small white box. With the other he started punching phone buttons.

On the mailing label of the box it said in blue letters: ARMSTRONG. And there was a return address in Wassau, Wisconsin.

Anyone who is a serious baseball card collector knows that Mr. Andy Armstrong of Wassau, Wisconsin, is one of the biggest baseball card dealers in the country. If not the biggest.

I opened the box.

"Arborville," Jim said into the phone. "I'd like the phone number for a party named Chuck Axelrod. I don't have his address. It's probably a new number."

I took out a bunch of cards and looked at them. They were like nothing I'd ever seen before. They were old black-and-white baseball photos. Fuzzy. Out of focus some of them. Maybe copied from old newspapers. Old pictures of old black ballplayers. I started spreading them out on the counter. I was looking into another world.

"Are these for sale, Jim?"

"Sure."

"How much?"

"Oh," Jim said into the phone. "Well, thanks anyway." He hung up. "Wouldn't you know it? He has an unlisted number. It's real smart having a celebrity for a league director. Now what? I've got it. Your old coach'll have his number. What's his name again?"

"Mr. Borker."

"His first name, Jason?"

"Bob. Robert, I mean. Jim, how much does—"

Just then a bunch of kindergarten-age kids came up to the counter with cards. Naturally, they all started talking at once.

"Jason, take those cards into the back room. You can spread out there."

"Thanks, Jim."

Between me, the kindergartners, and trying to get hold of Chuck Axelrod, Jim had his hands full.

"What've you got, gentlemen?" I heard him ask the kindergartners as I headed for the back room.

4

Truth in baseball cards? You bet. There they all were. The ballplayers Mr. Henry had told me about. One second I'd never heard of Cool Papa Bell. The next second I had him in my hands.

And there also was Josh Gibson. The greatest hitter who ever lived, according to Mr. Henry. Standing there looking at the camera, broad shoulders, roundish serious face, the word GRAYS across his uniform shirt. That had to be the Homestead Grays. It was all real. Everything that Mr. Henry was talking about.

And there were others too. Lots of others. Players I'd never heard of. And with great names. Bingo DeMoss, Bullet Rogan, Crush Holloway, Rats Henderson, Judy Johnson (a guy!), Jelly Jackson, Smoky Joe Williams, Double Duty Radcliffe. What was that nickname about?

There looked to be over a hundred cards in

this set. The teams each guy played for were on the backs of the cards. And it looked like each guy played for a whole bunch of teams. Mr. Henry had just mentioned a few. But there were also the Indianapolis Clowns and the Cuban X Giants and the New York Black Yankees and the Cleveland Buckeyes and the Newark Eagles and the Chicago American Giants. Jim had known about some of those too. There were the St. Louis Stars and the Baltimore Black Sox and the Baltimore Elite Giants. (Mr. Henry had mentioned the Elite Giants. Roy Campanella, he said, had played for them.) There were the Nashville Black Vols, the Brooklyn Royal Giants, the Bacharach Giants. So many teams named Giants. So many teams period, and till today I'd never heard of a single one of them.

How could I know so much about baseball and all of a sudden know so little?

There were no stats on the backs of the cards like you have on Ace or Topps or Donruss or Fleer. Just the team names and maybe little bits of information and stories. Like how fast was Cool Papa Bell? Mr. Henry said he was the fastest. And I guess he was. Because on the back of one of Cool Papa Bell's cards, Satchel Paige, who roomed with him on the Crawfords, said Bell was so fast he could turn off the light switch and be in bed before the light went out.

I laughed out loud at that one.

More names: John Henry Lloyd was the first superstar of the Negro leagues; Martin Dihigo played every position on the field; Rube Foster, a pitcher, won fifty-one games in 1902; Cannonball Dick Redding once struck out twenty-four men in a nine-inning game; Buck McHenry once struck out fifteen straight batters. I read the whole of the Buck McHenry card. Something had caught my eye.

McHenry was a powerful right-handed fireballer who pitched in the late 1930's. He pitched only three seasons for the Crawfords but won over ninety games. After several scrapes with the law, McHenry retired early from baseball and worked as a school janitor in Michigan. He later said he made more money sweeping than pitching.

I stared at the words "school janitor in Michigan." It couldn't be. I turned the card over. It was a fuzzy old black-and-white photograph of . . . of . . . My heart almost stopped. It was him. It had to be. It was Mr. Henry!

I just stared and stared. I don't know how long I looked at Mr. Henry, and then I grabbed the card and took for the main part of the store.

"Jim," I yelled, "I've got a coach for our team!"

40

I almost ran over three little kids looking at Detroit Pistons sweatshirts. I dodged between two mothers buying magazines. At the counter were two adult customers. I wriggled between them and shoved Mr. Henry's card at Jim.

"I know him, Jim. He lives here in Arborville. He could be the coach of The Grandstand team."

"I'll be with you in a second, Jason. What you really want, sir, is a Donruss favorite player pack. That would give you . . ."

Jim, I thought, stop with business as usual. This is important.

But Jim wouldn't be interrupted. Which told me he wouldn't have made a good coach for our new team in the first place. Baseball always comes first for a real coach. Like this morning when he was supposed to be minding the gym, Mr. Henry was outside watching our practice. And then inside the school he showed me how to take off out of the batter's box, how to run to first, even though my spikes had to be messing up his floor. Baseball came first with Mr. Henry.

While Jim did business, I looked again at Mr. Henry's picture. It was probably taken from an old newspaper. There were no statistics on the back. Just that little bit of information.

None of the cards had stats on the back. I wondered why not.

41

Oh, there was much I had to learn. When did the Negro baseball leagues start? Why did they start? What was life in them like? Why did they stop?

Mr. Henry could tell me. I wondered if he'd let us call him Buck McHenry. Well, not Buck McHenry, but Mr. McHenry.

It was clear as pie what he'd done. He'd changed his name by dividing it into two parts. McHenry became Mack Henry—the name on the custodian's closet at Eberwoods School.

No wonder his pitching motion had looked so good. And him saying he'd been there when Josh Gibson hit his home runs. He'd probably been on the field with him. Maybe he'd pitched the day Gibson had hit a ball out of Yankee Stadium.

Why had Mr. Henry quit baseball? The clue was right there on the card. *Scrapes with the law*. I wondered what that was about. Maybe he'd tell us. It was going to be fantastic having a baseball legend as a coach.

"Okay, Jason, what's the problem?"

"No problem, Jim. No problem at all. Truth in the cards, Jim? Isn't that what you're always saying? Well, do you see this card?"

"What are you going on about, Jayce?"

"This card is Buck McHenry. Did you ever hear of him, Jim?"

"Sure. He was a great right-handed pitcher in the old Negro leagues."

"Well, I've got news for you, Jim. Buck McHenry lives right here in Arborville. He's the custodian at Eberwoods School."

Jim started to laugh. So did another adult customer who'd come up behind me. "Department of wishful thinking," the man said.

Adults never believe something wonderful can happen.

"Just to start with, Jason," Jim said gently, "if Buck McHenry lived here in Arborville, we'd all know it. Secondly, he played in the 1930's. That was about sixty years ago. The odds are he's no longer alive. Now be a sport, Jason, and step to one side so I can earn a living."

I stepped to one side and waited while the man paid for his shirts. When he left, I said, "Jim, you don't understand. I saw Buck McHenry pitch in the corridor at—"

"Jason, I don't have time for nuttiness. Saturday's my busy day. And I've already put time in on our team."

"Our team? Does that mean . . . ?"

Jim grinned. "It sure does, pal. I talked to

43

Chuck Axelrod himself. Your old coach had his number. Axelrod seems like a nice guy for a celebrity. He allowed as how a baseball card store sponsoring a kids' baseball team might be the greatest idea since sliced bread. We're in, Jason. But we've got to move fast now. Practice games are already being booked between teams and we don't even have a team yet. Axelrod has a list of expansion players plus new kids in town who are eligible for our team. Two we know about already."

"Who's that?"

"You and his daughter."

"His daughter?"

"That's right. His daughter."

"But Mr. Borker said he had a son."

"Mr. Borker got it wrong. He has a daughter. Her name is Kim and he says she's a heckuva ballplayer."

"I doubt it."

Jim smiled. "Secondly, it's got to be a big plus having the league director with a special interest in our team. He wants us to have a team meeting at four o'clock today over at Sampson Park. Which means we don't have much time. All the kids on his list have to be called before four o'clock. I volunteered you to go over to his house and help his daughter make those calls. Here's the address. Put it in your pocket. 1800 Devonshire. Get on over there, Jason. And try to get as many fathers as possible to the meeting. One of them is going to have to coach our team."

"But that's what I'm trying to talk to you about, Jim. I've got a coach already. Buck Mc—"

"Jason, stop with this Buck McHenry nonsense and get over to Chuck Axelrod's house right now."

"Jim, would you *please* read this card? It says how Buck McHenry became a school custodian here in Arborville."

I pushed the card so close to Jim's face he had to read it. "It doesn't say anything about Arborville, Jason. It says he became a school custodian in Michigan."

"Isn't that close enough? And why did he change his name? He got into scrapes with the law. And how did he change his name? He divided it into two. McHenry became Mack Henry."

That shook Jim up a little. But he was stubborn. "Jason, it's impossible. I'll believe it when *he* tells me he's Buck McHenry, not you. And another thing." He tapped the card. "This picture is so old and out of focus it could be a picture of anyone."

"Jim, if I prove to you that Mr. Henry really is Buck McHenry, will you agree that he can coach our team?"

"Sure. And while you're at it you can prove to me that Sparky Anderson is my uncle. Meanwhile, get over to Chuck Axelrod's house."

"Jim, it's more important for us to get a coach first. And if we get Buck McHenry, we won't have to recruit kids. Every kid in Arborville will want to play for The Grandstand."

"Jason, I can't deal with you when you get like this."

"Jim, if Mr. Henry really is Buck McHenry, can I keep this card?"

"Jason," Jim said slowly, "if a school custodian in Arborville, Michigan, turns out to be one of the greatest right-handed pitchers who ever lived, you can have the whole set. And I'll throw in a poster of Isiah Thomas too."

"You mean that?"

"I do."

"Will you shake on it?"

"Gladly."

He stuck out his hand. And we shook on it. A whole bunch of customers came up then, which suited me fine. I had to get out of there right now.

The clock behind Jim said five minutes to

twelve. I was certain the adult basketball league ended at noon. I'd never make it to the school in time. I could probably catch him at home.

"Jim, can I look at the phone book?"

Jim didn't answer. He was busy. I slipped around the counter and grabbed the phone book.

It was kind of nice being behind the counter with him. Like we were running the store together.

There were a whole bunch of Henrys living in Arborville but only one Mack Henry—332 North Fourth Avenue. That was downtown, not far from the river. The other way from my house. I probably ought to call my folks and tell them I had to skip lunch for the sake of our new team.

No, better not. They'd get upset and tell me to come right home. Better to just head down to North Fourth Avenue and face the music later.

Which is what I did.

5

North Fourth Avenue is one of the oldest streets in Arborville. Two years ago our third-grade class visited a stone house there that had once been part of the Underground Railroad.

Before the Civil War, people in Michigan used to hide runaway slaves who were escaping to Canada. In that stone house there were trapdoors and tunnels and secret passageways. It was interesting and scary. It also made you realize what it was like for black people then.

332 North Fourth Avenue, where Mr. Henry lived, was in the same block as the Underground Railroad house. Only it wasn't half so big. It was a little white house with blue shutters and an aluminum awning over the front door. There was a flower garden in front and a white picket fence.

It was neat and tidy. The way you'd expect a custodian's house to look.

A sign hanging from the gate said: WEL-

COME. THE MACK HENRYS. I looked at it and hesitated. Suppose Mr. Henry said he wasn't Buck McHenry? Did I still ask him to coach?

Worse, suppose he didn't even remember me from this morning. Then what?

Stop, Jason, I told myself. You've come all this way. Go in and get it over with. Be tough.

I unlatched the gate and wheeled my bike in. I could hear a television set playing loudly inside the house.

I laid my bike down near the front steps and unlooped my mitt from the handlebar. That TV set was really blasting. Maybe his wife was hard of hearing. Maybe they wouldn't be able to hear the doorbell. If that was true, I could turn around and go home. Besides, my folks were probably worrying what had happened to me. The practice was long since over. I hadn't even had lunch yet. I might as well go home.

I took a deep breath and rang the bell.

Nothing happened. I rang it again. If no one came on this second ring, I was definitely going to leave. There was probably no one home. They'd probably left the TV on by mistake.

The door opened. A woman not much bigger than me looked at me with sharp eyes. "What can I do for you, young man?" Her voice was sharp too.

"Is Mr. Henry home?"

"He might be."

What kind of answer was that? Either he was home or he wasn't.

I must have looked flabbergasted because she went on, "It depends on what one wants to see Mr. Henry about. I'm his wife. You can tell me why you want to see him."

His wife and his bodyguard, it looked like. Maybe it had to do with those scrapes with the law. If so, I couldn't very well tell her I wanted to find out if he was Buck McHenry.

"Would you . . . uh, tell him that Jason Ross from Eberwoods School this morning is here?"

"Young man, if you left something inside the school, you are just going to have to wait till Monday. Mr. Henry is on his weekend and he's planning on going fishing this afternoon."

"I didn't leave anything, Mrs. Henry. I don't even go to Eberwoods anymore. I used to go there."

"Who's there, Jessie?" Mr. Henry's voice sounded over the TV noise.

Before she could answer, I shouted, "It's me, Mr. Henry. Jason Ross. From Eberwoods School this morning. You gave me a baseball lesson on how to run to first. Remember? I was delivering bases to you . . ."

Before I finished, Mr. Henry appeared behind his wife. He towered over her.

"Don't tell me you've got more bases to return, boy?"

I laughed. "No, sir. I just wanted to talk to you."

"What about?"

I looked at Mrs. Henry, who was looking very curious. Mr. Henry understood right away. "Jessie," he said, "would you go into his bedroom and get him to turn that TV set down so I can hear what's on Jason Ross's mind?"

"Mr. Henry, are you going to take up your Saturday with school business?"

"This boy doesn't go to my school"—which I'd already told her—"so it can't be school business. Go and tell him I hung the mattress out back and want him to try it out."

Try out a mattress out back? What was that about?

"It will take more than a mattress to get him moving, Mr. Henry."

She didn't understand he was only trying to get rid of her for a few minutes.

While they talked, I looked around the living room. Like the front yard, it was small and neat. There was a sofa and two soft chairs. They were each covered with clear plastic. There were little

51

tables with color photographs on them. There was a bookcase with books in it. And small statues of shepherds and people like that on top. On the walls were more color photographs. Mostly of a young man in an Army uniform.

I didn't see any sports photos or trophies. No pictures of Mr. Henry in a baseball uniform. Of course, if he'd had trouble with the law, the last thing he'd want around the house were pictures of himself in a baseball uniform.

After more talk, Mrs. Henry finally left the room and Mr. Henry turned to me. "How'd you find out where I live, boy?"

"The phone book."

In the other room the TV got turned down a little.

"You know, when I first started working for the schools, Mrs. Henry wanted me to have an unlisted number. I said no. She said kids'll be calling you. I said no they won't. Well, they called. But you're the first to actually come. All right, boy, what you want to talk about?"

He clearly wasn't sore about my coming over here. But still I hesitated about coming right out and asking him if he was the great Buck McHenry. For one thing, face to face, he didn't look as much like him as he had back in The Grandstand. I stuck my hand in my pocket and felt the hard edge of the card. It was reassuring.

"Spit it out, boy. It can't be that bad."

"No, sir. It's good really." I took a deep breath. "On my way home from Eberwoods, I stopped at The Grandstand. That's the baseball card store on the corner of State and Packard."

"I know where it is."

"Well, you remember some of the players and teams you were telling me about? The Pittsburgh Crawfords and the Birmingham Black Barons and Cool Papa Bell and—"

"I remember," he interrupted. He was wondering where this was all leading.

"Anyway, I asked Jim Davis who runs The Grandstand about those teams and he showed me some baseball cards from the Negro leagues and I found this card."

I whipped out Buck McHenry and gave it to him. My heart began to pound as he examined it. At first his expression didn't change. But then he smiled.

"Old Buck McHenry on a baseball card. Wonder of wonders."

It's him, I thought. It's him!

Mr. Henry turned his card over and read the stats side, which told how he had become a school custodian in Michigan. In the other room a car-rental commercial was now playing on the TV.

They always play the commercials louder than the program.

"That's an interesting card, boy, very interesting." He handed it back to me.

I cleared my throat. "Mr. Henry, are you Buck McHenry?"

He looked at me as though I was crazy. "Am I Buck McHenry? Boy, what on earth makes you ask a question like that? Buck McHenry was a great baseball pitcher." He laughed. "I wish I *was* Buck McHenry."

"Are you sure?" I persisted.

"Am I sure who I am?" The laughter got louder. It rose from inside his body and filled the room. "Jason, there've been times I wasn't so sure who I was. And times I wished I *was* someone else. But I'm pretty sure I've been Mack Henry for some sixty-eight years now."

He laughed so hard tears came into his eyes. It had to be an act. He was laughing too hard. It wasn't that funny.

"Your names are pretty close, Mr. Henry. McHenry and Mack Henry. And you never mentioned Buck McHenry this morning when you were talking about those old ballplayers."

He slapped his hand on his knee. "Boy, there's lots of ballplayers I didn't mention. Did I mention Sid Morton?"

"No, sir."

"Well, I'm not him either. Did I mention Bill Byrd or Cannonball Dick Redding or Mule Suttles?"

I shook my head. He was teasing me now. Trying to get out of it.

"I'm not any of them either."

I felt my face burning. I tried to keep my voice calm and even. "On the stats side it says that Buck McHenry became a school custodian."

"I saw that. I always wondered what happened to him. He quit while he had his best years ahead of him."

I bet you wondered what happened to him, all right. Well, I would have to take a chance now. It was risky, but I had to let him know I knew why he got out of baseball.

"It says Buck McHenry got into scrapes with the law," I said.

"I saw that." His eyes were twinkling. "All I can say is if you ever meet up with Buck McHenry, you might ask him what that was about."

"You think he's alive, Mr. Henry?"

We were playing cat and mouse with each other.

"Well, let's see. Old Buck played in the late 1930's and early 1940's. That would put him into his late sixties today. I bet he's alive and kicking. . . ."

Alive and kicking in Arborville, Michigan, I thought.

". . . Which is," he added softly, "more than I can say for most of those boys. Most of 'em died young and poor. And now some smart businessman has come along and figured a way to make them immortal and make himself a pot of money. Somehow that doesn't seem fair, does it, Jason?"

"I think it's right that there's baseball cards for them, Mr. Henry. I want to know about them."

"Well, maybe you've got a point there. Who else did you see on those cards?"

"Cool Papa Bell and Josh Gibson and Bullet Rogan and Crush Holloway and—"

"I saw Rogan play many times."

And played against him too, I thought. Well, I thought, I wouldn't push it. I knew. And he knew that I knew. And I knew that he knew that I knew. Stop. You're making yourself dizzy.

"Mr. Henry, can I ask you another question?"

"Not if you're going to ask me if I'm Josh Gibson too."

"No, sir. This is something else."

"Go ahead then."

"You remember this morning when I told you I was cut from my team?" He nodded. "And I told you there was going to be a new team?" He nodded again. "Well, Jim Davis who manages The Grandstand is going to sponsor the new team. Only we need a coach. I was wondering if you'd be our coach."

This time Mr. Henry was really surprised. He wasn't playacting now the way he had when I asked him if he was Buck McHenry. Now he didn't laugh. He stared at me.

"You'd be a great coach, Mr. Henry. You gave me a great baseball lesson this morning."

"Jason," he said solemnly, "you are nice to ask an old man to coach your ball team. I am flattered. But I'm too old to be coaching baseball."

"You're not too old, Mr. Henry! Connie Mack coached when he was over eighty. And Casey Stengel was still coaching when he was over sixty."

Mrs. Henry came back into the room. "I can't get him moving, Mr. Henry. You will have to do it."

I don't think Mr. Henry even heard her. He went on talking to me. "I don't know about Connie Mack and Casey Stengel, boy, but Mack Henry is too old. Still, it was nice of you to ask me. And I won't soon forget that."

"Ask you what, Mr. Henry?" Mrs. Henry was one of those people who always have to know what's going on. It would be hard if not impossible for Mr. Henry to have kept any secrets from her. I was sure she knew who he was.

"Jessie, young Jason Ross here has just offered me a job." He smiled, making a joke out of a serious offer.

"What kind of job?" Mrs. Henry didn't smile.

"He wants me to coach his Little League baseball team. That's what." Mr. Henry laughed.

Mrs. Henry didn't laugh. She turned to me and asked abruptly, "How old's your team, boy?"

What a question. Why would she want to know that? What did that have to do with anything? "It's brand-new, ma'am."

"No, boy. How old do you have to be to *play* on your team?"

"Oh. You have to be eleven. We're in the eleven-year-old league."

"Well," she said, turning back to Mr. Henry, "what are you going to do, Mr. Henry, or don't you see it yet?"

"You mean, am I going to coach a baseball team at my age?"

"That's *exactly* what I mean."

"The answer, Missus, is I am *not* goin' to coach a baseball team."

"If I were you, Mr. Henry, I'd think that over. If I were you, I would seriously consider the young man's offer."

They were funny the way they talked to each other. Like they were onstage in front of me. Which, in a way, they were.

"What are you trying to say, Jessie?"

"I'm saying, Mr. Henry, that we have an eleven-year-old grandson living with us who does nothing all day but watch TV. Or follow us around like a stray dog. How about that child following you to a baseball team and making friends with other children?"

So that was who was playing the TV set. An eleven-year-old grandson. Maybe he was a ballplayer.

Mr. Henry was silent.

"I'm going to fetch the boy right now," she said, and walked out of the room.

Mr. Henry's lips pursed and he blew one of his silent whistles. "Jason," he said softly, "I am beginning to regret I ever met you."

"But you'd be a great coach, Mr. —" I hesitated and then said boldly, "McHenry."

"Hey, you stop that McHenry foolishness right

now. My name is Mack Henry. Not McHenry. And don't you ever forget that."

"I promise I won't tell anyone."

"Jason," he said exasperatedly and then stopped. The door had opened. Mrs. Henry came back in followed by the kid my age. Except he was bigger than me. He was bigger than anyone on Baer Machine. Bigger than Cal Borker or Tug Murphy. He had wide shoulders. He was awesome for an eleven-year-old.

"Aaron," Mrs. Henry said, "this is Jason Ross, who used to go to the school where your grampa works. Jason, this is our grandson Aaron Henry, who has moved up from Memphis to live with us."

"Hi," I said to Aaron Henry, who sure looked like a ballplayer.

Aaron Henry stared at my Baer Machine shirt and my mitt and then he looked down at the floor. He was shy. And with muscles like that.

"Aaron," Mrs. Henry said, "Jason Ross has just said hello to you. I want you to say hello back to him, boy."

It was an order. "Hello," Aaron Henry mumbled. He still wouldn't look me in the eye.

I wondered what was wrong.

6

Mrs. Henry broke the silence that followed.

"Back in Tennessee," she said, "Aaron Henry was supposed to have been a very good baseball player."

"Is he on a team now?"

We were talking as though Aaron Henry wasn't there.

"Why don't you ask him yourself?"

It felt odd but I repeated the question to Aaron Henry. "Are you on a team in Arborville?"

Still not looking at me, Aaron Henry shook his head.

"You've got a tongue, Aaron Henry—use it," his grandmother snapped at him.

"I ain't on a team," Aaron Henry mumbled.

"I'm *not* on a team," she corrected.

"I'm not on a team," he repeated.

"That's better." She turned to me. "Aaron was a pitcher on his baseball team in Memphis. Now what I want to know is, Jason, could your team use a good pitcher?"

"Aw, Grandma," Aaron said.

"*Now* you can be quiet, boy. I'm talking to Jason. Jason, can your team use a very good pitcher?"

"Could we ever! We'll be going nowhere unless we get a good pitcher. We're an expansion team." I felt embarrassed. "We're mostly rejects from other teams. We'll need a good pitcher bad." Aaron was looking at me. "Would you come on our team and pitch for us?"

"No," he said.

Bango. Just like that. No. I was stunned by how quick he said it and how final it sounded.

There was a heavy silence. Finally Mrs. Henry broke it. "Well," she said, giving her husband a sharp look, "are *you* going to speak up?"

All this time Mr. Henry hadn't said a word. Like he didn't want to get involved.

"What do you want me to say, Missus?"

"You *know* what I want you to say, Mr. Henry."

You could tell he did and also that he didn't want to say it. But she kept looking daggers at him, and finally he turned to Aaron, who had gone back to staring at the floor.

"Look at me, boy," Mr. Henry ordered.

Aaron looked at him. Grampa and grandson

looked at each other. They looked alike, I thought. And in a few years Aaron would look exactly like Buck McHenry on the baseball card.

"Listen to me, boy. Jason Ross here has biked across town to ask me to coach his new baseball team. If you're willing to play on it, I'm willing to coach it. What do you say?"

My heart leaped up. From nowhere to everywhere. From nothing to everything. It was a genuine twofer. We get a coach and a pitcher in one fell swoop. But—and it was a big but—if we didn't get one we wouldn't get the other. Come on, Aaron Henry, I prayed, say yes.

But Aaron Henry shook his head. "I told you, Grampa. I don't want to play baseball anymore." His voice was husky. His eyes were pleading with his grandfather. I didn't get it.

"You did tell us that, boy. But I thought maybe you'd change your mind. I guess I know why you won't, though. You don't think Jason here can catch your fastball. Well, I got news for you, boy. I saw Jason catch this morning, and he sets up behind the plate just like Roy Campanella used to. Why don't you get a baseball out of the box in the closet and throw a few to him? He's got his catcher's mitt with him. See if he can't catch you."

"Grampa, you're just trickin' me."

"Enough!" Mrs. Henry snapped. She reached over and grabbed Aaron's ear between her thumb and forefinger. "Up you go. You're not going to watch TV all day long in my house. You are coming with me right now."

She twisted his ear hard, making him stand up.

"Grandma, that hurts."

"That's nothing compared to what I'm going to do to you if you don't start behaving yourself." She looked triumphantly at Mr. Henry. "Aaron Henry and I are going to find a baseball, and then he is going outside and playing with Jason. Isn't that right, Aaron Henry?"

"Ouch," Aaron Henry said as she yanked him out of the room by his ear. Seconds later Mr. Henry and I heard boxes being moved about somewhere and her saying, "Keep on looking, boy. It's there somewhere."

"I guess you're wondering what's going on here, Jason," Mr. Henry said to me.

I nodded. I was.

"The boy is grieving. He's mourning."

As he said those words, Mr. Henry's face changed. His eyes, his mouth, began to twitch. Like the features on his face were about to come apart. Like he was going to cry. I winced. I couldn't picture Buck McHenry crying. I didn't want to be around if that ever happened.

He didn't cry though. He pulled himself together. He blew his nose into a handkerchief. And looked at me.

"Last month in Tennessee, Aaron lost his mama and his papa and his brother in a . . . car crash. He . . ."

He stopped, unable to continue. I didn't understand what he'd said. Lost? In a car crash? What did that mean? And then it hit me. Lost meant dead. Aaron's mother and father and brother had been killed in a car crash.

That was just awful. Your mother and father and brother. And Aaron Henry's father must have been Mr. Henry's son. This was terrible. I shouldn't be here. It was crazy of me to come here today.

He must have understood what I was feeling. "It's all right, boy," he said gently. "I'm glad you came now. Maybe you can help us make Aaron his old self again. You see, the reason he doesn't want to play baseball anymore is because that was what he was doing when his family was killed. He was playing in a Little League game in Memphis. That was why he wasn't in the car with them. That's why he's alive today."

He blew his nose again and wiped it. "A baseball game saved the boy's life. But for what? To grieve and grieve and grieve. The doctor down there says he feels guilty because he's alive. I tell him we've all got to come back from what happened. I tell him but he doesn't listen. He doesn't even hear."

In the other room Mrs. Henry said, "That's the box right there. The ball's in it and your glove too. You fetch that box out."

"The doctor down there thought a change of scenery would do him good, so his grandma and I brought him back up here to live with us. He says he doesn't want to live up here. You've got to live somewhere, I tell him, and what you're doing isn't living anywheres. He says he wants to go back to Tennessee. I tell him all you're going to do down there is what you're doing up here, and that's nothing. Watching TV is nothing. I tried to get him to throw a ball with me, but he won't do that. I thought maybe he'd throw a ball to a mattress. So when I came home from the school today, I hung a mattress against the shed in back." He shook his head. "But he won't do that neither."

Mr. Henry looked at me. "Maybe you can help me with the boy, Jason?"

I nodded. I'd help you with anything, Buck McHenry, I thought.

"Go out back and see if he'll pitch to you."

"I'd be glad to, Mr. Henry."

Mrs. Henry came back in the room. "I got him as far as the porch steps. He won't go any farther."

"Jason's going to try and throw a ball with him, Jessie."

"Are you? Well, boy, bless your heart. But you got to go slowly with him. You see—"

"I told him, Jessie. He knows."

Her eyes filled with tears. He gave her his handkerchief. She started to cry. "It's . . . through the . . . kitchen."

I got out of there fast. I went down the hall, through a kitchen, and out onto a screened-in porch. It was a big porch with large wicker chairs, a card table, and lamps. There was a door to the outside. And steep steps leading down to the backyard. The backyard was long and narrow. At the far end was a shed, and hanging down on the side was the mattress. Mr. Henry had painted a bull's-eye on it.

Aaron Henry was seated on the bottom step. Next to him on the step was a glove and a ball.

The screen door clicked shut with a sharp noise, but Aaron didn't turn around. I sat down next to him.

"How're you doing?" I asked, and knew right

away it was a dumb thing to ask. How *could* he be doing? His father and mother and brother were dead.

"Wanna see my mitt?"

I held up my catcher's mitt. He glanced at it. And looked away.

"I was backup catcher on Baer Machine but I'll be the starting catcher on The Grandstand team. That's the team your grampa's going to coach, Aaron."

His lips curled scornfully. "My grampa doesn't know anything about baseball. How's he going to coach a team?"

"The heck your grampa doesn't know anything about baseball. He was only one of the greatest baseball pitchers who ever lived. He won ninety games in three years."

"You crazy or something? What're you talking about?"

Although I'd promised Mr. Henry I wouldn't tell anyone who he really was, I had to make an exception here. His grandson had a right to know!

"I'm talking about this," I said. I started to take the Buck McHenry card out of my pocket and then I thought, No, use it in trade.

"I got your grampa's baseball card right here." I patted the pocket.

"Who you foolin'?"

"I'm not trying to fool you. I got a baseball card with your grampa's name and picture on it."

"Let's see it."

"I'll trade you."

"I don't have any baseball cards."

"I'll trade for something else."

"What?"

"I'll let you look at your grampa's baseball card if you pitch to me and let me see how good a pitcher you really are."

"Now I know you're fooling. Grampa sent you out here. I bet you don't even have a card in your pocket."

"I do too."

"Let's see."

"All right, I'll show you a little bit of it."

I took the card carefully out of my back pocket and showed him just enough so he could see it was a genuine baseball card.

"And you're saying my grampa's on that card?"

"I'm not saying. I know he is. I even showed it to him."

That stopped him. He thought about it.

"What's your name again?"

"Jason. Jason Ross."

"Okay, Jason. You go down by Grampa's dumb

mattress. I'll pitch to you. Then you're going to show me his card. Right?"

"Right!" I ran down to the other end of the yard and stood in front of the mattress with the bull's-eye on it and looked back at the house and the back porch that was supported by iron poles. To the right of the porch was a window, and in it Mr. and Mrs. Henry were watching us. Aaron couldn't see them. He had his back to them.

"You want to warm up?" I called out.

He nodded. "I haven't pitched in a while."

He threw some easy tosses at me, and while I couldn't tell yet if he was a pitcher, I could tell he was a ballplayer. He had a nice easy motion.

"How long's it been since you threw?" I asked. I was just trying to make conversation, but it was a pretty dumb thing to say. Pitching was what he had been doing when his family was killed. I shouldn't be reminding him of that. That was a subject to stay away from.

He didn't answer right away, and I said, "I'm ready. You ready?"

"Yeah," he said. "I'm ready."

"Okay," I said and squatted down, "fire away."

The moral of what happened next is that "fire away" is a dumb thing to say when you don't know who you're asking to fire away.

Aaron went into a slow windup that reminded me of his grampa. He was Buck McHenry on a smaller scale. The same motion, the same high kick, and then he fired the ball at me.

Only this wasn't an imaginary ball in a corridor at Eberwoods School. This was a real baseball coming at me like a bullet. I ducked at the last split second and the ball whistled past me and smacked up against the mattress. It made a smashing sound. And, for all I knew, a hole in the mattress.

I stared at Aaron Henry. Never in my life had I seen a kid my age throw that hard. Not Cal Borker, not Tim Corrigan, not Manny Fernandez who pitched for the Bank team. If Aaron Henry pitched for The Grandstand, we'd beat Baer Machine any day of the week and the Bank team twice on Sundays.

He was talking to me.

"What'd you say?" I said.

"How come you didn't catch it?"

"Are you crazy? It would've broken my hand. I'll need a sponge in my glove to catch you. No, correct that. Two sponges."

He saw I was serious. And he laughed. He stood there and laughed. I didn't mean to make him laugh but he laughed. Mr. and Mrs. Henry heard that laugh. I saw them smile at each other.

I fetched the ball and went up to him. "You're a pitcher all right, Aaron. We'll be a winning team with you. You want to see your grampa's baseball card?"

His eyes were alive. Alive and interested. "Yeah. Let's see that card."

I took the Buck McHenry card out of my back pocket and handed it to him. As I did so, I remembered my promise to Mr. Henry not to tell anyone. I looked up at the back window. They weren't there now. I guess they didn't want Aaron to think they were spying on him. Maybe it would still be all right. Maybe they wouldn't mind my telling Aaron. It was in a good cause.

"That ain't my grampa. That's someone named Buck McHenry."

"Your grampa's name *was* Buck McHenry. What he did was chop his last name in half when he quit baseball. McHenry became Mack Henry."

Just as that detail had shaken Jim Davis, it also shook up Aaron. But then he looked doubtful. "It don't look like my grampa."

"It don't look like him *now*. But it looked like him then."

"My daddy would've told me if Grampa was a professional baseball player."

"He probably didn't know. It was a secret. Read the other side." It irritated me that he would doubt his own grandfather's greatness.

"There," I said, pointing to the words on the stats side. "It says he became a school custodian in Michigan. And right below it says why. He quit baseball because he had scrapes with the law."

Aaron was silent. He turned the card over and looked again at the picture.

"It still don't look like him," he said, but he was beginning to weaken.

"The picture's out of focus. Jim Davis at The Grandstand says most of the pictures of the Negro league baseball stars are out of focus. Ask him if you don't believe me."

By "him" I meant Jim Davis.

"I will," he said, and took off for the house like an Olympic sprinter.

"Where're you going?" I yelled.

"To ask Grampa like you said," he yelled, waving the card over his head without looking back.

"I didn't mean your grampa," I shouted. "Stop!" But it was too late. He was in the house already.

Mr. Henry was going to be very angry with me, I thought.

7

"Whoa. Slow down, boy. You're talking too fast for an old man."

Mr. Henry and Mrs. Henry were seated on the plastic-covered sofa looking up at Aaron, who was pointing at the Buck McHenry card.

"Jason says you used to be a famous baseball player, Grampa. And your name was"—he looked at the card—"Buck McHenry. Were you him, Grampa?"

I couldn't bear to look at Mr. Henry.

To my surprise, though, he laughed. "No, boy, I'm not Buck McHenry, but I sure did like seeing you throw to Jason. You threw that ball hard."

"Real hard," I said.

Aaron turned to me. "He's not Buck McHenry and he can't coach your team."

"Wait a second, boy," Mr. Henry said. "Where does it say a man has to be named Buck McHenry in order to coach a baseball team?"

74

"Aw, Grampa."

"Don't 'Aw Grampa' me. This country is full of folks coaching baseball teams whose names aren't Buck McHenry."

Aaron gave me back the card. "You were just tricking me to play baseball."

"What's wrong with playing baseball, boy?" Mrs. Henry said.

"Aw, Grandma."

"Don't you 'Aw Grandma' me either. I'll twist your ear off if you go on behaving like a hermit. You should be out making friends up here." She looked at Mr. Henry. "As for you, sir, I think it's high time you owned up to who you were."

"What are you saying, woman?"

"I'm saying it's time to own up to who you are, Buck McHenry."

I gulped. So did Aaron. Mr. Henry stared at his wife. Talk about being betrayed.

"Jessie, stop talking nonsense," he said.

"I'm not talking nonsense, Buck McHenry. I want your grandson to start living again, and if it means admitting who you are, then you should do that. What is it going to cost you, Buck McHenry?"

Mr. Henry was silent. He didn't look at Aaron or me. I guess when you've had a new name for years, you don't take the old one back easily.

Those scrapes with the law must have been more than just scrapes. Maybe Buck McHenry had killed someone. But I couldn't believe that. Not Mr. Henry.

"Tell him, Buck," Mrs. Henry insisted.

Mr. Henry remained silent.

"Mr. McHenry," she said, "if you want to go on eating meals in this house, you will admit to the boy who you are."

She meant it, too. Mr. Henry looked helpless. He didn't want to do this. But he had to.

"Boy," he said, "look at me."

Aaron looked at him.

"You want me to be Buck McHenry? I'll be Buck McHenry."

But the way he said it was all wrong and Aaron shook his head. "It's okay, Grampa. I didn't think you were him anyway."

"For God's sake, tell the boy clean out," Mrs. Henry snapped.

There was a silence. Then Mr. Henry said, "All right, boy. I *was* Buck McHenry. But it was a long time ago. Before you were born. Before even your daddy was born. And it's all over now."

But it wasn't over at all, I thought. It was just beginning and it was wonderful! I couldn't restrain myself. I clapped my hands.

No one even looked at me. Aaron turned to

his grandmother. "Is it true, Grandma?"

"Yes, boy, it's true. Your grampa doesn't like to live in the past, but sometimes you have to. Now, I've had enough of this foolishness. I'm going out front to do some gardening. You behave yourself, Buck," she said as she went out the door.

"You're not makin' this up, are you, Grampa?" Aaron asked. He was still suspicious.

"No, he's not," I said.

"How come you never told anyone?" Aaron slid onto the floor at his grampa's feet.

"How come I never told anyone?" Mr. Henry frowned. "I guess I didn't think it was worth telling. That's how come."

"But you're on a baseball card. That's worth telling."

"Not to me, boy."

"Didn't you ever tell Daddy?"

"No."

"Why not?"

"Because like I just told you, it all took place before he was born. It took place before I even met your grandma."

"But you told her."

Mr. Henry smiled. "Had to. A man can't keep secrets from his wife. Especially your grandma." He chuckled.

Aaron's face was serious. "Can I see the card again, Jason?"

I gave him the Buck McHenry card and then slid down next to him on the floor.

Aaron read the stats side again. "It says you were a great pitcher, Grampa. It says you won ninety games in three years."

Mr. Henry laughed. "Don't believe everything you see in print, boy."

"Did you or didn't you, Grampa?"

"I probably did."

"Mr. uh—" I began and stopped. I didn't know what to call him. Henry or McHenry?

He knew what I was worrying about. He smiled. "You keep calling me Mr. Henry, Jason. That's my name now."

"Okay, thanks. Mr. Henry, can I ask you some questions?"

"What kind of questions?" He sounded suspicious. I didn't blame him. He hadn't wanted to admit who he was and now I wanted to know even more.

"How come there are no stats on the backs of these cards?" I asked.

He looked relieved. He probably thought I was going to ask him about those scrapes with the law. But I wouldn't do that. That would be really mean. You'd have to be a TV reporter, the kind that ask a family whose house has just burned down how they feel.

"How come there's no stats on the cards?" he repeated. "Well, that's easy to answer, Jason. Who was going to keep statistics in those leagues? There wasn't any money to pay someone to keep records. There wasn't even money to pay players. Most of those boys played for the love of the game and carfare home. And they were lucky if they got carfare."

He kept saying "they," not "we." He was still being cautious, but at least he was talking about the old days. This was the most exciting thing that had ever happened to me. Talking with a living baseball card.

"How come there were Negro leagues in the first place, Mr. Henry?"

"That's history, Jason. You've got to know your history."

"I don't know it."

"Me neither," Aaron said.

"Well, you both heard of Jackie Robinson, didn't you?"

"Sure," we said.

"Well, till Robinson broke the color bar they wouldn't let colored ballplayers into regular organized ball. I'm talking about major *and* minor leagues. Oh, a couple of fellows'd sneak in from time to time as Indians and Cubans. Like Chief Bender. But Charley Grant, who was a fine second baseman, couldn't make it as an Indian even though John McGraw, manager of the New York Giants, gave him an Indian name—Chief Tokahkoma. That was a long time ago."

"Before you played, Grampa?"

"Yep, boy, even before I played. Fact is, from the very beginning white folks wouldn't let black folks play baseball with them."

"How come?" I asked.

"How come? How come folks don't like other folks just because the color of their skins is different? How come? I don't know how come. You've got to ask a white man that. Ask your father how come."

"I will."

"Then you tell me what he says, because I don't know. All I know is that when baseball leagues first started way back after the Civil War, they didn't want black men playin' with white men. That's when it started. Lincoln freed the slaves but he didn't free them to play ball."

"Were they any good?" Aaron asked.

"Were who any good?"

"The slaves."

"Slaves didn't play baseball," Mr. Henry said crossly.

"So who are we talking about, Grampa?"

"I'm talkin' about what came afterward. When there were colored ballplayers better than the best white ballplayers. Men like Gibson and Satchel Paige and before them John Henry Lloyd, Rube Foster. Better than any white players."

"Better than Babe Ruth?" Aaron asked.

"That's right, better than Babe Ruth."

"Josh Gibson hit a ball out of Yankee Stadium once," I said to Aaron. "Babe Ruth never did that."

"How do you know, Jason?"

"Your grampa told me. Mr. Henry, did you know Satchel Paige personally?"

Mr. Henry leaned back on the couch. "I knew them all, boy."

"Was he as great as they say—Satchel Paige?"

"Better. There were those who said Smoky Joe Williams was better, but I never saw him pitch. Matter of fact," he said, chuckling, "I never saw much of Satchel's pitch either. Especially his fastball. He called it 'trouble' or 'jump ball.' 'Trouble' because that's what it gave to batters. And 'jump' cause it took a little jump at the end and disappeared."

"Where'd it go?" asked Aaron.

Mr. Henry laughed merrily. "Into the catcher's

glove, boy. That's where it went." We laughed too.

"Who was the best all-around player in the Negro leagues, Mr. Henry?" I asked.

He didn't take long to give an answer. "John Henry Lloyd was the best baseball player ever lived, Jason. Colored or white."

"His card was in that set," I said.

"Was he better than Josh Gibson?" Aaron asked.

"Not as great a hitter. No. Not that. But a greater ballplayer. Greater than Ty Cobb. Greater even than Honus Wagner. I bet you heard of Honus Wagner, Jason."

"Sure. He was in the original Hall of Fame. A mint-condition Ace 1911 Honus Wagner is the most valuable card around. One sold last year for over a hundred thousand dollars."

Aaron's mouth fell open. "A hundred thousand dollars? For a baseball card?"

"That's right."

Mr. Henry smiled. I couldn't tell whether he believed me or not. But it was the truth.

"Would you two like to hear a little story about the great Honus Wagner *and* John Henry Lloyd?" Mr. Henry said.

I inched up closer. I loved getting the inside scoop like this. Mr. Henry hadn't just read about these guys. He had played with them. He was one of them!

"One day a reporter in his newspaper column called John Henry Lloyd 'a black Honus Wagner.' Someone asked Honus Wagner to comment on that. And you know what Mr. Honus Wagner said?"

"What did he say?" we asked.

"He said, 'I am proud to be compared to John Henry Lloyd.' That is exactly what the great Honus Wagner said. 'I am proud to be compared to John Henry Lloyd.' Now what does that tell you about John Henry Lloyd?"

"That he must have been better than anyone who ever played ball," I said, thinking it also told you something about Honus Wagner. He must have been a good man besides being honest.

"John Henry Lloyd was the best," Mr. Henry said.

"I bet he wasn't better than you, Grampa," Aaron said. His eyes were shining.

Mr. Henry smiled. "He was a lot better than me, boy."

"But you could've pitched in the big leagues if they'd let you, Grampa."

"I like to think so, boy."

"Can I ask you another question, Mr. Henry?"

"You do enjoy asking questions, don't you, Jason?"

"I guess," I laughed, a little embarrassed. "My dad says I'm going to be a lawyer like him. Lawyers ask lots of questions. Except they're only supposed to ask questions they know answers to."

"What're they asking for then?" Aaron said.

"To trap people in court."

"That's ugly," Aaron said.

Mr. Henry laughed. "I agree with you, boy. I think it's better to ask questions because you don't know the answers. Not because you do. How else are you going to learn anything? Go ahead, Jason. You were asking . . ."

It was wonderful. Now Mr. Henry really wanted to open up about the old days. I'd done him a favor. I inched up closer. So did Aaron.

8

"How come the Pittsburgh Crawfords were called Crawfords?" That was my question.

"Who were they?" Aaron asked me.

"Best black team ever brought together," Mr. Henry said. "That's who they were. I pitched for them. So did Paige. Gibson was our catcher. Cool Papa Bell played in the outfield and Judy Johnson played third base."

"Judy?" Aaron said.

"Short for Judah, though his first name was Bill."

That didn't make much sense, but I didn't want to interrupt.

"On that same team was Oscar Charleston. And who else? Oh, Jimmie Crutchfield, Rap Dixon, and Double Duty Radcliffe."

"I saw his card. How'd he get a nickname like Double Duty, Mr. Henry?"

"The way it happened, Ted Radcliffe pitched

the first game of a doubleheader and won it. And caught the second game. Some reporter gave him that name right then and there. Because he did double duty. Let's see, who else was there? Oh, lots. We jumped around a lot. Mostly we didn't belong to a league. Just went around the country, playing who'd ever play us. We played hard, though we might ease up on a poor team. A batter'd hit a ball down to third with no one on base and Judy Johnson'd whip it to Sam Bankhead at second and he'd whip it to Oscar at first and they'd still get the runner out at first by a step. That's how good that Crawford infield was."

"What'd they do that for?" Aaron asked.

I was about to ask that too. It seemed like a really unprofessional thing to do.

"To have fun," Mr. Henry said gleefully. "To make a close game out of a poor one."

"I bet they wouldn't've done it if Cool Papa Bell was running out that hit," I said.

"No, we wouldn't've done that, Jason. Just to start with, Cool Papa was on our team. He was our center fielder. But if he was on an opposing team, well, no one, not even our boys, would fool around like that. The only way you could get Cool Papa out on a ground ball was, let's say with no one on he hits a ground ball to third. Well, if the third baseman had his wits about him, he'd fake throwin' to first, fake throwin' to second, and then tag Bell out as he came slidin' into third."

I laughed. Aaron, grinning, said, "He was fast all right."

"Fast isn't the word to describe Cool Papa. He was a strong breeze goin' by. You felt him, you didn't see him.

"Oh, they were all good, you know. Born to run, born to hit, throw, catch. You didn't have to teach them. There was no one to teach them. There was no coaching. There was no spring training. You put on a uniform and you started playing. You learned by playing. No one brought you along. They figured if they paid you, you were good enough. And they were good enough. We'll never see them again. The Crawfords, the Homestead Grays—"

"How did the Homestead Grays get their name?" I asked.

He hadn't told me yet how the Crawfords got their name, but maybe he didn't know. Ballplayers don't always know stuff like that. They're too busy playing.

"Homestead Grays got their name from the old Homestead Steel Works outside Pittsburgh. We all lived around there."

"It was like Little League then," I said. "Having teams named after businesses."

"Well now, I never thought of that. You could be right, boy. Of course we didn't do much philosophizing about our profession. We lived to play ball. Teams came and teams went. Sometimes a fellow would play for three or four teams in the course of one season."

"How could he do that, Mr. Henry?"

"He'd jump teams. Everyone did it. Paige did it all the time before he finally settled down with the Kansas City Monarchs. He'd go where the money was. And the money was there for him. He made a lot. Of course it's nothing compared to what they make now, but it was a lot for then. Josh Gibson didn't make half as much as Paige and we didn't make half as much as Gibson. The owners made money, all right. But there was no players' union. No lawyers. No agents. Just the idea that someone would pay you to do what you loved to do, that was enough."

"Did you have all-star games, Mr. Henry?"

"Yes we did, Jason. There was an all-star game between the Negro National League and the Negro American League."

"Were you in one, Grampa?"

"More than one, boy."

"Did you get the wins?"

"I expect I did. You could look it up. They kept records on the all-star games."

"Was it fun or was it hard being in those leagues, Mr. Henry?" I asked.

Mr. Henry smiled. "As I remember, it was a little bit of both. Sometimes it was hard and sometimes it was fun and sometimes it was fun and hard at the same time. Going around the country, especially the South, we played in some hostile ball parks and with some hostile fans. The home clubs paid the umps, so when you were a visiting team you often got cheated and that was hard to accept. But . . . we had fun too. Everyone could play just about any position, though of course you were apt to be better at one position than another. The managers all played. We didn't have more than thirteen, fourteen players on some teams." (Like Little League again, I thought.) "You got hurt, you played. You made do with what you had. You made something out of nothing. There were no whirlpools, no clubhouses, no hot tubs, no fancy hotels. You slept in old buses, in old cars, in ratty hotels. Unless you were Satchel Paige, you didn't get rich. But there you were, playing ball, being paid to do what you'd do for nothing, and that's the best job anyone can have."

"I'm going to have that job," Aaron said quietly.

"That so?" Mr. Henry looked amused. "And who's going to give it to you, boy?"

"The big leagues."

Mr. Henry chortled. "Maybe they will, but first you've got to earn it. And I don't know about that. I've got to see how good you are."

"Oh, he's good all right, Mr. Henry. He throws harder than anyone," I said.

"That right? Well, only thing I saw this boy throw till today was stones in a river while I was trying to fish. In those old leagues we had boys not much older than him throwing complete games, and throwing them harder than full-grown men."

"I could pitch in those leagues, Grampa," Aaron said firmly.

"Put that in the past tense, boy. You'd have a hard time finding one of those leagues now. They are *long* gone. When Mr. Jack Roosevelt Robinson went up to the Brooklyn Dodgers in 1947, that was the beginning of the end for the old black leagues. After that lots of black ballplayers came into white ball. And black fans, they went to the big white ball parks to see how their boys did in the major leagues. It was integration that ended the old Negro leagues."

"Did that make you sad, Mr. Henry?"

"No, Jason, that didn't make me sad. That's progress. And progress means money and fame for the new black ballplayers. The Jackie Robinsons, Willie Mays, the Monte Irvins, Hank Aarons, Frank Robinsons, Bob Gibsons. Sure, sometimes I look back and wish I could have been born a little later. Me and Josh and Satchel and Cool Papa and Oscar and Judy and Buck Leonard and oh, there's so many that could have been stars. Martin Dihago, we haven't even talked about him and he was one of the great ones. He was from Cuba. And Smoky Joe Williams before my time and Dandridge who almost did make it to the big leagues. Well, Satchel used to say, never look back. You've always got to look ahead. I like being me now. I like being who I am now, what I am, where I am. Of course," he added with a chuckle, "at my age I don't have a baseball future."

"Sure you do, Grampa," Aaron said. "You're going to coach our team."

Coach our team? I jumped up.

"We've got to get moving," I said. "All we've got so far is a sponsor and a coach. We're supposed to have a team meeting today over at Sampson Park."

"Grampa, we have to go to the meeting," Aaron said.

"I'm planning on fishing this afternoon, boy."

"Grampa. Please."

"Well, I guess if I'm going to coach a team, I better meet up with them. But you two have to promise me something first."

"What's that?"

"You both have to promise you won't tell anyone who I used to be. Especially kids. People in this town, they've known me for thirty years as Mack Henry. I don't want to confuse them. To everyone around here my name is still Henry. Mr. Mack Henry. You've got to forget about my ever being Buck McHenry."

"But Grampa, kids should know who you were." Aaron looked unhappy. I didn't blame him one bit.

"Unless I get your promise, boy, I'm not coaching your team."

"I promise not to tell kids," I said. I'd already promised once about not telling who he was and broken it. But I hadn't told any of the kids. That was a promise I could still keep.

"Aaron?" Mr. Henry asked.

"I promise," Aaron said reluctantly.

"What time's the meeting, Jason?" Mr. Henry asked.

"Four o'clock. At Sampson Park. But I don't know how we can have a team meeting. We don't even have a team yet. I was supposed to call up kids on Chuck Axelrod's list—the expansion players—and tell them about the meeting. The list's at Chuck Axelrod's house."

"Chuck Axelrod? The Channel 4 man?" Mr. Henry's eyes opened really wide.

Here we go again, I thought. The power of TV. If there was another Chuck Axelrod living in Michigan, no one knew it.

I nodded. "He lives in Arborville. They asked him to be director of the eleven-year-old league. His daughter's going to be on the new team. I'm supposed to help her make phone calls." I looked at Aaron. "You want to come help with the phone calls?" I wasn't sure I wanted to be alone with Chuck Axelrod's daughter. She could be a real jerk.

"Can I go with Jason, Grampa?" Aaron asked.

"Of course you can, boy." Mr. Henry looked pleased.

"I'm on my bike, Mr. Henry. Does Aaron have a bike?"

Aaron shook his head.

"Yes, you do too have a bike," Mr. Henry said to him. "There's an old bike of your daddy's in the shed. I kept it oiled. Go get it, boy."

For a second I wondered if maybe riding a bike of his father's would sort of scare Aaron, but it didn't. He got up and ran out of the house.

"Isn't that somethin'," Mr. Henry said, his eyes following Aaron as he left.

"It's great."

"I better make sure he doesn't mess up my shed."

Mr. Henry went out the back way and I went out the front door. Mrs. Henry was working in the flower garden on her hands and knees. She looked up as I came down the steps. She was looking into the sun. She shaded her eyes with one hand to see me better.

"Mr. Henry's going to coach and Aaron's going to play, Mrs. Henry. And Aaron's coming with me now to help me make phone calls. We don't have a lot of time and we've got to recruit kids for the team."

"Well, well," Mrs. Henry said, "think of that. One second he doesn't know anyone. The next he's going to meet a lot. Well, we have something to thank you for, Jason Ross."

I felt myself blushing. "I'm the one who should be doing the thanking, Mrs. Henry. You helped us get the great Buck McHenry as our baseball coach."

"That's right. I did. Tell me something, boy.

Did Mr. Henry say he didn't want you telling folks about him?"

"Yes, ma'am."

"Well then, you be sure you do as he says. It's got to be a secret."

"Oh, it will. We won't tell a soul. I promised. And Aaron promised too."

Just then Aaron and Mr. Henry came around the side of the house pushing Aaron's dad's bike. Aaron looked happy.

Mrs. Henry gave him a severe look. "You're going into society now, Aaron. You behave yourself, you hear?"

Aaron grinned. "I will, Grandma."

"You keep an eye on him, Jason."

"I will, Mrs. Henry."

Mr. Henry laughed. "They'll be all right, Jessie."

"See you at four at Sampson Park," I shouted at Mr. Henry as we took off.

"I'll be there," he called after us. "And remember you aren't goin' to tell anyone, especially kids. . . ."

Those were the last words we heard as we took off down the block.

Funny how you remember something like that.

9

Aaron and I rode up North Fourth Avenue, up Huron, then Washtenaw. We went past a lot of buildings I could point out to him. Starting with the big old stone house on North Fourth Avenue that had been part of the Underground Railroad.

Then City Hall on the corner of Huron and Fifth. Then the *Arborville News* building. I detoured us past some of the university's athletic buildings and then we headed up Washtenaw, going by the big fraternity and sorority houses.

Aaron took it all in, looking from one side of the street to the other.

"This town at all like Memphis?" I asked him.

"Memphis is bigger."

"I know. If we had a minor-league team, it'd only be Class A. Memphis has got a Double A team. The Chicks."

"How do you know something like that, Jason?"

"Baseball cards. Heck, everything I know is from baseball cards."

Aaron hesitated. Then he said, "What're you going to do with my grampa's card?"

"Give it to you."

That just popped out of me. I'd never given away a card before. You're not supposed to *give* away cards. If you want to get rid of one, you trade it. Even duplicates. Especially duplicates. You've got to treat cards like a major-league ball club treats players. Trade them, sell them, and if they get too shabby, dump them. But out of nowhere I'd shot my mouth off and given away a baseball card. One I didn't even own yet, as a matter of fact.

"Thanks, Jason," Aaron said softly.

We pumped up the sidewalk past the First Presbyterian Church. It was uphill here. Aaron wasn't breathing hard and it was a one-speed he was pedaling.

"Heck," I said, trying to make myself feel better about the freebee, "I'm gonna get the whole rest of the set for nothing. Jim Davis said he'd give it to me for free if your grampa turned out to be Buck McHenry."

"We're not supposed to tell anyone, Jason."

He was right. I hadn't thought of that. How was I going to get the set for free then? Wait.

I'd made the bet with Jim before I'd made the promise to Mr. Henry. And, at that, I'd really only promised not to tell kids. I was in the clear.

I told Aaron all that. And added, "Jim didn't believe me. All he said was that he had to hear it himself from your grampa before he'd believe it."

"Well, Grampa won't admit it to him, Jason."

"Then I'll buy the set. How much could it cost anyway?"

"I wish Grampa would admit it. I wish he'd tell everyone who he is. I don't know why he's bein' like that."

I knew why. It had to do with scrapes with the law. Mr. Henry was probably still on the run. But I couldn't very well tell *that* to Aaron.

"Well, maybe he doesn't want to be bothered by folks. If the kids in Arborville found out he was the great Buck McHenry, they'd be pestering him to death for his autograph. And the kids who go to Eberwoods would be the worst. They'd be after him all the time in the halls even. He'd never be able to do his job."

Aaron thought about it. He nodded. "I guess you're right. You know what bothers me most, Jason?"

"What?"

"That my dad and mom and Louis aren't ever

goin' to know. I wish there was some way I could tell them."

A chill ran down my spine as he said those words. The last thing I wanted was to set him to thinking about his family and get him all sad and closed up again. I had to change the subject fast.

"We only got about two blocks to go. You getting tired?"

"No. My daddy had a good bike."

"That's Devonshire up there," I said quickly, "the street coming in on the left."

"We have to cross?"

"Yeah."

There was a lot of traffic on Washtenaw. It's a state highway. Finally lights stopped the traffic down at Hill and Washtenaw and up at Brockman and Washtenaw. No cars were coming. We ran our bikes across the street to Devonshire Road.

Now the neighborhood began to change. At Devonshire Road begins the fancy part of Arborville. Big houses, big lawns, no sidewalks. That's how you can tell a rich part of town. No sidewalks.

Of course, it's how you can tell a poor part of town too, no sidewalks. But the streets in the poor parts of town aren't paved and the houses are small and all you ever see in front of them are pickup trucks and motorcycles. Here Mercedes and BMWs were parked on the circular drives off the streets with no sidewalks.

1804 Devonshire, two houses up from the corner, was a big house with a big lawn in front. There were all kinds of trees and bushes and flower beds.

We got off our bikes and walked them quietly up a long curving brick walk. I think we were both a little intimidated. The house was big. Halfway to it, Aaron turned to me. "Your house this big, Jason?"

"Are you kidding?"

I couldn't tell if he was disappointed or not. I think he wanted my house to be this big so maybe I'd know how to behave here. I didn't know any more than he did.

We finally got to the front door. We laid our bikes down and confronted it. The door was big and thick. There were ivy vines growing around a tiny stained-glass window toward the top.

"This is like a castle," Aaron whispered.

"No, it's not. Castles have moats and draw-bridges. This place doesn't even have a doorbell."

Aaron pointed at a lion's head sticking out on the door. "That's the doorbell," he said.

It was a door knocker in the shape of a lion's

head. Lion's whiskers fanned out into a solid bar you were supposed to yank up and let go.

"Go ahead, do it," I said.

"You do it," he said.

"Let's both do it."

"Okay."

We reached out together and pulled the lion's whiskers up. It was solid. It would bang hard when we let go.

"One, two—" Aaron began.

The door suddenly opened. We were holding on to the door knocker so tightly that we almost got pulled into the house. We caught ourselves on the sides of the doorway.

A girl our age stood there looking at us. She had short dark hair and wore a sweatshirt that said BINGHAM FARMS.

"What do you boys want?"

"Does, uh, Chuck Axelrod live here?" I asked.

"Yes."

"I'm supposed to see him."

"Are you Jason Ross?"

"Yeah."

"If you're Jason Ross, you were *supposed* to be here an hour ago," she said.

It was pretty snotty the way she said that. I decided to go on the attack. "I was busy getting my new team a coach. Are you his daughter who's *supposed* to play on the team?"

"I'm *going* to play."

There was no "supposed to" in her reply.

"What's your position?" Aaron asked in a friendly tone.

"Infield. I can pitch too. Are you on the team?"

"Yep." Aaron grinned. "And my grampa's goin' to coach us."

"Your grampa?" She sounded doubtful.

"Hey," I said, "his grampa only happens to be—" I caught myself just before I let out the secret—to a kid!

"Go ahead, tell her," Aaron whispered.

"No!" I said.

"Tell me what?"

"Nothing."

"Kim," a familiar voice called out from inside the house, "who're you talking to?"

It was the voice of Channel 4 sports. I'd know it anywhere.

"It's Jason Ross and another boy, Dad."

"Bring 'em in, honey."

She nodded to us and opened the door wide. We stepped into a large front hall.

"This way," she said. After we went through the hallway, we followed her into a room big enough to have a basketball game in. Three on three. There was hardly any furniture. The walls were bare. No pictures. There were no shelves or bookcases. It didn't look very lived in. There was a big TV set in one corner. That and one chair was about it.

After that we went through another mostly empty room. We could hear Chuck Axelrod talking to someone.

"You ever get lost in this place?" I asked her.

"Once," she said.

Aaron laughed.

We went down two steps into another hall that was lined with cardboard cartons.

"You just move here?" Aaron asked her.

"About a month ago."

"Me too," Aaron said.

They were both new to town. I hadn't thought of that till now.

Chuck Axelrod's voice was getting closer.

Finally we entered a large office-den. This was where the furniture was: chairs, tables, a couch, and pictures. Lots of pictures.

At the far end, seated behind a desk, was the man himself, looking just like he did on TV. Hair falling over his forehead, horn-rimmed glasses, large pop eyes behind them, and a mouth that was always moving.

He was talking into the phone, and as he talked he motioned for us to sit down. Sit down where, I wondered? Every chair had something on it: papers, magazines, video cassettes, audio cassettes. His desk was piled high with papers and cassettes. There were two phones on his desk, one red and one black. There was a computer, a printer, a photocopier, a fax machine, a VCR, and an audio cassette player. The walls were covered with black-and-white glossy photos of famous athletes.

"Jimmy," Chuck Axelrod said into the phone, "did I ever not deliver when I said I would?"

I looked at the pictures on the wall. They were pictures of Tigers, Pistons, Red Wings, Lions. All the Detroit teams. There were pictures of former players, current players, and, as far as I could tell, each picture was autographed to Chuck Axelrod from so and so.

It was just the opposite of Mr. Henry's little house where, if he wanted to, he could have put up pictures of a hundred great players he'd played with. Not just interviewed. And Mr. Henry didn't have a one. He just had family pictures.

"Jimmy, you worry too much," Chuck Axelrod said. "Stop asking me because I don't know yet. Just make sure I have a crew standing by. Tony's if I can have them. If nothing happens I'll make something up. No, no. For the next hour I'll be tied up with Kim's baseball team. I know, I know. But it's something I have to do. Listen, I've got visitors right now. I'll get back to you in two minutes."

He hung up and winked at us. "My producer is getting nervous about tonight's show. I lost a live interview with Sparky and now I've got five minutes to fill. Okay, which of you is the famous Jason Ross?"

"Him," his daughter said, pointing to me.

"Jason, you did good work getting a baseball card store to sponsor the new team. But you're late getting here and time's of the essence. This afternoon we've got to—where did I put the darn thing?"

"What're you looking for, Daddy?"

"That list of names. I had it on my desk. If you'd come when you were supposed to, Jason . . ."

Kim Axelrod slipped out of the room.

"I was getting us a coach, Mr. Axelrod," I said.

"Who? Your father? That couldn't have taken that long." He peered under a stack of video cassettes.

"No, sir. I got Aaron's grandfather."

"Who's Aaron?"

"Him. My friend."

Chuck Axelrod looked up from his search at

Aaron. "Your grandfather know anything about baseball, Aaron?"

His condescending tone got to me.

I spoke up. "His grampa was only one of the greatest right-handed pitchers in the history of the old Negro leagues."

Aaron looked shocked. "You told," he whispered.

"Your grampa said especially not kids," I whispered back. But I'd done wrong. He'd said not to tell anyone. If I could have yanked those words back into my mouth, I would have. But it was too late. Chuck Axelrod had stopped looking for the player list and was gazing at the two of us with intense interest.

10

"Are you making a joke, Jason?"

A lot of grief would have been saved right then and there if I'd answered "yes" to that question. But that would have been lying. I may shoot my mouth off, but I'm not a liar.

"No, sir. I'm telling the truth."

Chuck Axelrod turned to Aaron. "That a fact, son? Your grandfather played in the old Negro leagues?"

"Yes, sir."

"What's your grandfather's name?"

Aaron hesitated. He shot me a should-I-tell-him? look.

No, you shouldn't, I tried to message him with my eyes. What we've got to do is change the subject. Something I was becoming very good at.

"Do you know about the old Negro leagues, Mr. Axelrod?" I asked.

"Of course I know about the Negro leagues," Chuck Axelrod said. "I did a show on them once. I did an interview with Cool Papa Bell at Cooperstown when he was inducted into the Hall of Fame. Let's get back to—"

"I didn't know Cool Papa Bell was in the Hall of Fame."

"Well, he is. And so are Josh Gibson and Paige and John Henry Lloyd."

I was impressed with Chuck Axelrod. He wasn't just TV show biz. He knew his stuff. "Is Double Duty Radcliffe in the Hall of Fame too?"

"Never heard of him." (And that, in a way, made him even more legit. He was honest.)

He was looking at Aaron. "What's your grandfather's name, son?"

When Aaron didn't answer, Chuck Axelrod shook his head disgustedly. "You kids are making jokes while your team is running out of time."

"No, Mister," Aaron said, "Jason and me aren't jokin'. My grampa was a great pitcher. Only we're not supposed to tell anyone."

"Is that so? And why aren't you supposed to tell anyone?"

"Because he changed his name a long time ago. That's why," Aaron said.

Chuck Axelrod laughed. "The story gets better and better. But kids, I don't have time for jokes." He got down on his hands and knees and started going through papers that had fallen off his desk.

Aaron looked at me. I could tell he wanted to tell Chuck Axelrod his grandfather's name in the worst way. Well, we'd gone this far. Besides, not telling made us look bad. Chuck Axelrod thought we were fooling around.

"His name was Buck McHenry," I said.

Chuck Axelrod looked up. "Buck McHenry?"

"Yes, sir. Did you ever hear of him?"

"Buck McHenry pitched for the Pittsburgh Crawfords. If I recall correctly . . ." Chuck Axelrod sat back up on his chair, "Buck McHenry pitched on the same team with Satchel Paige. He was supposed to have thrown as hard as Paige, but he quit early in his career."

"And went to work as a school custodian in Michigan. You got the card, Aaron?"

"You still got it, Jason."

And so I did. In my pocket, where it was beginning to get creased. I whipped it out and handed it to Chuck Axelrod.

"That's Buck McHenry. And he's Aaron's grampa."

Just then Kim Axelrod came back into the room with a sheet of paper in her hand. "I've got it," she said.

Her father didn't even look at her.

"On the back is where it says about him working as a school custodian," I pointed out.

"I see it."

"Well that school's here in Arborville. It's Eberwoods School, where I used to go."

Chuck Axelrod looked over the top of the card at us. "Did *he* tell you he was Buck McHenry?"

"Yes," we said.

"How do you know he wasn't putting you on?"

"Because," I said, "he didn't want to admit it in the worst way. Aaron's grandma made him confess." For a brief moment I thought about mentioning the scrapes with the law, but I didn't. He surely had spotted it on the card. He could put two and two together just as well as me.

"Dad," Kim Axelrod said.

"One second, honey. What's your grampa's name now, son?" he asked Aaron.

"Mack Henry," Aaron said softly.

Chuck Axelrod saw it right away. McHenry to Mack Henry. His eyes gleamed, just the way Jim Davis's had when I told him there was going to be a new team in the league. They were each like dogs after a bone. I could understand Jim

110

Davis's interest. But I was pretty slow figuring out Chuck Axelrod's. Maybe you've figured it out already. I hadn't.

"Buck McHenry is your grampa," Chuck Axelrod repeated slowly. He was trying to be cautious and it wasn't in his nature.

"Who's Buck McHenry?" Kim Axelrod asked.

"His grampa," I said.

"My daddy's daddy," Aaron said.

Warning signal again. We've got to stay away from that.

Before I could change the subject, Chuck Axelrod asked Aaron, "What's your grampa's phone number?"

"Mr. Henry's going to be at the team meeting at four at Sampson Park," I said.

"That's fine, but I've got to know ahead of time that he is who you and he say he is."

Why did he have to know it ahead of time?

"You know your grampa's phone number, Aaron?"

"Mr. Henry's not home now," I said. "He was going fishing till the team meeting."

Chuck Axelrod looked exasperated. "All right, is your grandma home?"

"Yeah, my grandma's home," Aaron said.

"So what's the phone number?"

"I don't know."

Chuck Axelrod was getting irritated.

"Aaron just moved here," I explained, and wondered if I should explain further that Aaron lived with his grandparents. But then he'd ask why and that would bring up the car crash in Tennessee. And that had to be a secret. A real secret. Compared to that the secret of Buck McHenry was nothing. Absolutely nothing.

But Chuck Axelrod was already punching buttons on the red phone.

"Will someone tell me what's going on?" Kim Axelrod asked.

"Aaron's grampa was Buck McHenry, a famous ballplayer in the old Negro leagues," I explained.

"That's fine, but we've got to start calling kids. I've got the list."

"Let's see it," I said.

"A party named Mack Henry living in Arborville," Chuck Axelrod said into the phone.

The first few names on the list were familiar, all right. They were terrible ballplayers.

"Do you know any of them?" Kim asked.

"All of them. And they're all lousy."

"There's no answer at your grandparents' house, Aaron," Chuck Axelrod said.

"Grandma's probably outside still working in the garden, isn't she, Jason?"

"I'm sure."

Chuck Axelrod's fingers tapped impatiently on a video cassette while the phone in his ear kept ringing busily. He was coming to a decision. He hung up, picked up the phone again, and punched more buttons. I hadn't the slightest idea who he was calling now.

"Dad," his daughter said.

"What is it, honey?"

"I've got the list. You gave it to me."

"Then for Pete's sake, start calling. Carol, let me talk to Jimmy. It's urgent."

"I knew we were wasting time," Kim Axelrod said. "Come on, let's go."

"Jimmy . . ."

Aaron and I started to follow her, but Chuck Axelrod's next words stopped us in our tracks.

"Jimmy, I've got the missing story for tonight's show. . . ."

If someone had had a camera and taken a picture of Aaron's and my faces just then, it would have shown two stunned kids.

"Are you guys coming?" Kim Axelrod called from another room.

We were not going anywhere. We were frozen.

"Gold, Jimmy, gold just fell into my lap. A fantastic local story . . ."

"Jason," Aaron whispered, "he's goin' to—"

"I know."

There was no way we could stop him, either. Even if we wanted to, which deep down neither of us did. Something had gone into motion that no human being could prevent. Chuck Axelrod was waving the Buck McHenry card around as he talked. At one point he saw us still there. "Don't worry about this card, kids. I won't lose it. I've got to hold on to it for a little longer. I'll get it back to you. No, Jim, I'm talking to a couple of Kim's teammates. This is what we're gonna do. I'll do a voice-over for the game shots and coaching shots. I'll do an interview with some kids, with our star—he's an old man, a guy who played in the old Negro leagues, which you are too young to know anything about but you will when I'm done. We can lay his interview over some stills too. In fact, I've got the prize still right here in my hand. Would you believe a baseball card, Jimmy? A baseball card!"

Aaron turned to me. "He's goin' to tell the whole world about my grampa."

"I guess so. I'm glad."

"Me too," Aaron said.

"There's nothing we can do about it now. We better go help with those phone calls."

"Yeah. Let's go help her."

What was going to happen was going to happen. It was like the sun coming up in the morning or the rain falling or the wind blowing. It was life! It was natural! It was good!

We ran to catch up with Kim Axelrod.

11

We ended up in a family room that was as big as the living room. No furniture but, sure enough, more telephones. One red and one black.

"You got phones in every room?" Aaron asked her.

"Just about."

"Bathrooms too?" I said, kidding.

"In one of them." She was serious.

Aaron whistled. "How many bathrooms you got anyway?"

"Four."

"Wow."

"That's a lot of toilet paper," I said. I didn't think Aaron should be impressed by lots of bathrooms.

"We don't *use* every bathroom," she retorted.

"Jason just means you got a big house," Aaron said gently.

She shrugged. "Where we used to live was

bigger." She wasn't bragging. Just stating a fact.

"Where'd you used to live?" I asked.

"Birmingham."

"That's near Detroit," I explained to Aaron. "Aaron just moved here from Tennessee."

"Where in Tennessee?" she asked him.

"Memphis."

"We used to live in Nashville. My dad worked in a TV station there before we moved to Michigan."

"I've never been to Nashville."

"What's the sweatshirt stand for?" I asked her.

She looked down at the BINGHAM FARMS across her chest. "That was the name of my school in Birmingham."

Birmingham was less than fifty miles from Arborville. "Why'd you move to Arborville?"

"My parents got divorced."

"So?"

"So in the settlement my mom got the house and furniture and my dad got me."

Ouch, I thought. That had to hurt.

There was a silence. It's hard to know what to say after someone says something like that. But Aaron found the right words. "Your dad got the better deal," he said softly. He really was nice.

Kim Axelrod blushed. "Thanks."

"Hey, your folks divorcing is no big deal around here," I said. "Half the kids I know in Arborville, their folks are divorced." That was true, too. Tug's folks were divorced. So were Kevin's and Silver's and Diaz's. And then there was Aaron with no folks at all. But I wasn't going to get into *that*.

"Okay," Kim Axelrod said, getting business-like again, "what about these kids?" She handed me the player list.

"Well, like I said, they're all pretty bad. This first guy, Gerald Kofer. He played for Bob's Texaco. His teammates called him 'Glue' because his bat never left his shoulders."

Aaron laughed. Kim didn't. "What about the others?"

"Well, there's Andy van Gasse. He played for Garnet Realtors. He's a fat kid whose father makes him play. Victor Perles collects baseball cards and can't hit the side of a barn. Norman Fahler throws like a girl."

Oops. Dumb thing to say. She yanked the paper out of my hand. "I can throw as good as you, if not better," she snapped.

"Bring your glove to the park and we'll see."

"I will."

"Good."

The day a girl could outthrow me in baseball was the day I'd hang up my shoes. But I had the sense not to say that out loud. That would be like pouring gasoline on a fire.

"Anyway," I said, "all the guys on that list are rejects."

"Aren't you a reject too? In fact, I think your name's on that list. Here it is. Jason Ross, Baer Machine, catcher."

I felt my face get red. "Okay, so I'm on the list, but I'm a lot better than those guys. I was backup catcher to Tug Murphy, who's the best catcher in the league. Tug'll probably be a major leaguer when he grows up. And I can hit okay. These guys can't hit, field, run, throw. They're hopeless. H-O-P-E-L-E-S-S." I spelled it out for her.

"So what should we do? Not call them?" she said.

"Call them. It's better to play and lose than not play at all."

"That's a great attitude."

"I'm just being realistic."

"You don't know how good I am. Or him." She pointed to Aaron.

"Oh, I got an idea how good he is all right.

He was an all-star in Memphis."

"I made the all-star team in Birmingham last year."

"Girls' league."

"Boys' league."

"Girls *here* play softball."

"They do in Birmingham too, but I like hardball. Have you asked enough questions? Are we going to call these kids or not? We're supposed to have a team meeting in about an hour."

The timing was impossible, I thought. But I guess we had to give it a try.

"Okay, give it to me. I'll call Glue first." As I took the list from her, one of the telephones rang.

The three of us stared at it. "That's our home phone," Kim said. She picked it up. "Hello." Pause. "Yes, he's here." She handed the phone to me. "It's for you."

"Me? You're kidding. Is it a kid?"

"A man."

It had to be Jim Davis, I thought. He was the only one besides Mr. Henry who knew I was supposed to come here.

"Hello."

"Jason . . ."

It was my dad. My heart sank. I knew I should have called my parents from The Grandstand.

Or from Mr. Henry's house. They had expected me home after practice. They must be worried about me. How had he even found out where I was?

"Dad, I'm sorry."

"Jason, we've been trying to track you down for hours. I called Mr. Borker, Tim Corrigan, Tug Murphy. They're worried about you too. In fact, they're probably running around now looking for you. I finally had the sense to try The Grandstand. Jim thought you might be at this number. Jason, what's going on?"

"Dad, the most exciting thing has happened. The most fantastic thing in the world. Did Mr. Borker tell you I got cut?"

"Yes, he did. That's why they're worried about you."

That stopped me. I hadn't put those two things together. I guess the Baer Machine guys thought that because I got cut from the team, I might want to throw myself in the Huron River. That was kind of funny.

"I'm okay, Dad. Better than okay. I'm great. I'm on a new team. The Grandstand. Jim's going to sponsor it."

"I know all this, Jason."

"What you don't know, Dad, is I got the team a new coach. A great coach. Dad, it's unbelievable, but Mr. Henry, the custodian at Eberwoods School, do you remember him, he's going to be our coach. Only he's not really Mr. Henry. Who he is really is Buck McHenry, one of the greatest pitchers who ever lived. He pitched with Satchel Paige in the old Negro baseball leagues. In three years in those leagues he won ninety—"

"Jason, stop," Dad said quietly but firmly. "We want you to come home for lunch. It's almost three o'clock. Your mother and I are having a hard time remembering what you look like."

"Dad, what I'm trying to say is I can't come home just yet. Aaron and me and Kim Axelrod have got to recruit players for a team meeting at four at the park. Aaron's my new friend. He's Mr. Henry's grandson. And Kim Axelrod is Chuck Axelrod's daughter. She's going to be on the team. We've got to make a whole bunch of phone calls right away."

"Make your phone calls from here, Jason. Bring your friends here. Jason"—Dad's voice got very gentle—"don't make me come get you."

When my father's voice gets gentle is when he is most serious.

"I'll be right home," I said, and hung up.

"I've got to go. I haven't had lunch yet. I'll make the phone calls from my house while I'm eating. Unless you guys want to come with me and call too."

"But we've got two phone lines here," Kim said. "We could call different kids at the same time."

"Your dad's always on one phone. And besides, I *got* to go. You and Aaron can make the calls from here, if you want."

"It'd be better if you were there. They know you. In case they want to know something we don't know about. I'll ask my dad if I can go to your house."

"Aaron and I are on bikes. Do you have a bike?"

She nodded.

"We'll see you out front then. Don't forget to bring your glove. We can go over to the park from my house. We live real close."

She took off.

It wasn't so easy getting out of the Axelrod castle. At one point Aaron and I wandered into the kitchen, which was as big and bare as the rest of the house. They must eat out a lot, I thought. Finally we made it to the front hallway and out the door to our bikes. We didn't have long to wait for Kim. She came pedaling around the house, biking over the lawn. She had a ten-speed boy's bike. A fielder's glove was looped around the handlebars.

"Let's go," she said, and shot past us down the walk and over the curb and into the street, where she made a tight little circle and yelled, "Which way?"

"Left," I yelled back.

Aaron shook his head, smiling. "She's somethin', isn't she?"

"So far she's all talk," I replied.

He laughed. We shoved off. We pedaled hard, trying to catch up with her. But we couldn't. She was all talk and a ten-speed bike, I thought, as she zoomed ahead of us.

12

My mom, Jean Ross, is an artist. Her idea of excitement is to go off with her sketchpad and draw pictures of wildflowers. When she comes to my games, she usually draws pictures of us. At the end of the game she always asks, "Who won?"

She's pretty laid back, and if you hang around her long enough you get pretty calm too.

"Hello, stranger," she said to me as I came into the house with Aaron and Kim.

"I'm sorry, Mom. I lost track of the time. This is my friend and teammate Aaron Henry."

"Hello, Aaron," Mom said. "I'm glad to meet you."

"And this is Kim Axelrod. She's on the team too."

"But isn't a friend," Mom said, and laughed. "Hello anyway, Kim." She turned to me. "Dad told me you have phone calls to make, Jason.

I'm afraid you're going to have to eat lunch first."

"If it's okay with you, Mrs. Ross, Aaron and I can call while Jason eats," Kim said.

"It's not okay with me," I said. "I'm making the first call."

"Why should you make the first call?"

"To show you guys how to do it."

"What makes you think we don't know how?"

"I know these kids. I know how to talk to them."

"That's all well and good, Jason," Mom said. "But first you're going to eat a sandwich. So please sit down." She turned to them. "Have you two eaten?"

"Yes, ma'am."

"It's just peanut butter and jelly and we have a lot of it."

"No, thanks," they said.

"Please feel free to change your minds." She got a carton of milk out of the refrigerator.

"Please, Mom, no milk," I said.

"What do you mean, no milk?"

"Milk cuts down your wind."

"Oh?" Mom said, pouring out a big glassful. "And where did you hear that?"

"On the back of a Diamond Stars card."

Kim Axelrod laughed. "You believe the stuff on the backs of those cards?"

I was surprised. Diamond Stars are old cards. Put out by the National Chickle Company in the 1930's. Not too many kids today know about them.

"You heard of Diamond Stars?"

"I've got some. They have hints about how to pitch, catch, steal, bunt. They came with Chicklets."

"So you collect cards?"

"Yep."

"Eat, Jason," Mom warned.

I took a big bite of peanut butter and jelly. "Howmanycardsyougot?" I asked, my mouth full.

"About thirty thousand."

Aaron whistled. "She's got thirty thousand cards, Jason," he said.

"I heard, I'm not deaf." I washed the peanut butter and jelly down with milk. I burped.

Mom said, "Jason, you're going to get sick if you eat that fast. Please chew your food."

"It's quality not quantity that counts in cards," I pointed out to Aaron. "I've met kids at card shows who have two hundred thousand cards." I burped again and pounded my chest. "What's your most valuable card?"

"An Ace 1952 Mickey Mantle."

That was too much. "You've got *that* card?"

"Signed too."

That was the card I'd been telling Mr. Henry about at Eberwoods this morning. When he asked me why Mantle was worth more than Mays. That Mantle card was worth over $2500. I couldn't begin to guess what it was worth with Mantle's signature on it.

"Do you know Mickey Mantle?" Aaron asked her. He was awed. So was I, for the moment.

"No. My dad did an interview with him and asked him to sign the card."

"If your father wasn't a sportscaster, you probably wouldn't have anything," I said.

"And if your father wasn't a lawyer, you wouldn't be talking that way." A new voice had entered the conversation.

I spun around. Dad was standing there looking amused. He had on gardening gloves. He'd been working in the backyard. I wondered how long he'd been listening to us.

"Who are your friends, Jason?"

I introduced him to Kim and Aaron. He looked at Aaron with interest. "You must be the one whose grandfather is Buck McHenry?"

"Yes, sir," Aaron said proudly.

"Have you heard of Buck McHenry, Dad?"

Dad got himself some coffee and joined Mom at the dining-room table. "A few years ago someone published a history of the old Negro leagues.

Buck McHenry was in there along with Cool Papa Bell and Josh Gibson and Satchel Paige."

"I didn't know you knew about those guys."

"I don't know an awful lot. But Grampa told me that when he was a kid he saw the Homestead Grays play in the old Polo Grounds."

"My grampa Ross lives in New York City," I explained to Aaron. And to Kim, I explained, "The Homestead Grays were a team in the old Negro leagues."

"I know that. I've got a set of Negro League Baseball Stars."

"No, you don't," I said. "There are no Negro league sets. No Ace, Topps, Fleer, Donruss—"

"I'm not talking about a set you buy with gum. Andy Armstrong in Wisconsin printed his own set last year. He sent one of the first batches to my dad."

I stared at her. Wherever I went, I met this girl coming back.

"Look," she said, "we've only got a half hour before the team meeting. Can we start calling kids now? Can we use this phone, Mrs. Ross?"

"Of course, Kim."

"I'm making the first call, remember?"

"You'll do nothing, Jason, until you finish your milk," Mom said.

"But you gave me so much."

"Drink it slowly."

"Aaron, you want to start?" Kim asked.

Aaron shook his head.

"Okay, I'll do it. Do we tell kids about your grampa being famous?"

"Sure," Aaron said.

"We can't do that," I said.

"Why not?" Kim demanded.

"Because we promised his grampa we wouldn't tell kids."

"But you told my father. He'll tell the whole world."

"That's different."

"I don't get the difference," Aaron said.

Dad laughed. "You don't get it, Aaron, because there isn't any difference. All it means is that your friend Jason is on his way to being a politician. Leaking information rather than giving it."

"A promise is a promise," I said, my face turning red.

"All right, we won't tell," Kim said. "The first kid on the list is Gerald Kofer."

"The first and the worst," I said.

"Maybe we can make him better," she snapped. She dialed Kofer's number.

"Can I speak to Gerald Kofer, please?" she said. "Oh. Do you know when he'll be in? I see.

Well, if he does come back, would you tell him there's going to be a meeting of his new team at Sampson Park today at—oh." She listened. "Well, if he changes his mind. Okay. Thanks anyway." She made a face as she hung up.

"His mother said he was so upset about being cut that he's never going to play baseball again."

"Good news for everyone," I said. "You're 0 for 1. You bat next, Aaron."

Aaron looked grave as he took the paper from Kim and read: "Andy van . . . ?"

"Gasse," I said. "And that's what he's full of too."

"That's not very nice, Jason," Mom said.

"Jason doesn't like anyone," Kim said. She was miffed, being 0 for 1.

"Excuse me," Aaron said softly into the phone. "Is Andy in? Oh. I'm, uh, Aaron Henry. I'm calling about our new baseball team. We're having a team meeting at Sampson Park today at— Oh—sure, that's okay. If you change your mind we uh— Sure. So long."

Aaron hung up. He looked embarrassed, as though it was his fault. "He says he was only playing baseball because his father was making him. He says his father has quit making him."

I finally finished my milk. "You're batting zero too, Aaron," I said cheerfully. "Now I'll show you guys how it's done. And why I wanted to go first. You can't just *ask* them to be on a new team. You've got to *sell* the team to them. Listen and learn."

"Pride goeth before a fall, Jason," Dad warned. He and Mom were sitting at the dining-room table watching us. I guess we were better than a floor show to them.

Next on the expansion-player list was Victor Perles. He was a tall, skinny kid who collected baseball cards. He wasn't a bad kid but a dreadful ballplayer. I dialed his number. I knew how to approach Victor.

The phone rang. And rang. And rang and rang and rang. No one was home.

Kim, grinning, nudged Aaron. "Jason can't even get it to answer. That's like not getting into the game at all. You never left the bench, Jason. My turn." She held out her hand for the phone.

What a snot. Well, I'd show her. "Hello," I said to the ringing in Victor Perles's house.

Kim stopped grinning.

I kept a straight face. "Victor, this is Jason Ross," I said to absolutely no one. "I'm calling for your new team—The Grandstand. That's right. The baseball-card store. Isn't that great? And we're going to get free baseball cards from

Jim. Win or lose. Pretty good deal, huh?"

"Is that right?" Kim whispered to Aaron.

"I don't know," Aaron said.

"This afternoon, Vic," I went on, "we've got a meeting at Sampson Park. Bring your glove, because our coach'll want to look us over. We've got a great coach, by the way. He's Buck McHenry, one of the greatest right-handed pitchers of all time. He pitched with Satchel Paige in the old Negro leagues. He's even on a baseball card."

"Wait a second," Kim said, "you said we couldn't tell kids. You're changing the rules. That's not fair."

That almost broke me up. If she thought that wasn't fair, she should only know what I was doing now.

I went on merrily. "We've also got some great players, Vic. Buck McHenry's grandson is going to pitch for us. He was an all-star pitcher in Tennessee." I hesitated and then I couldn't resist it.

"We've also got a girl on the team who, if she's as good as she says she is, is going to sign a pro contract before the season ends. She—"

That was as far as I got. Kim grabbed the phone from me. *Ring, ring, ring* it went in her ear.

"Just as I thought," she yelled. "There's no one there."

"You didn't think that at all," I said, breaking up. "I fooled you." I howled with laughter. Aaron realized what I'd done and started laughing too. Mom and Dad were laughing. Pretty soon everyone but Kim was laughing.

"I . . . fooled . . . you." I was laughing so hard my stomach hurt. I could hardly talk. I could hardly breathe. I began to feel nauseous. I could feel the milk I'd drunk so fast rising in my esophagus to smite me. I put my hand on my chest and tried to force it back down.

"You fooled me all right," Kim said. "We've got about fifteen minutes to call eleven kids. And you fooled me for two of those minutes. You think that's so smart?"

I stopped laughing. She was right. I'd been fiddling while Rome was burning.

"Okay," I said. "No more gags. I'll make three calls. You three. Aaron three. We'll go fast. Agreed?"

They nodded.

After that we went fast. Too fast. Only one of my kids was at home and he was sick and not interested. Aaron called three kids. One wasn't home and the other two didn't want to play ball this summer. Kim called three and none of them were home. That left two more kids to call. Kim called them both. Neither were there.

Well, we made all the calls in less than fifteen minutes. We also didn't recruit a single player for The Grandstand team. We had a great pitcher, a great sponsor, a coach who was a living legend. But no team.

I felt nauseous all over again. And this time it had nothing to do with milk.

13

"I better call my dad," Kim said gloomily. "He's got a camera crew coming in from Detroit."

I explained to Mom and Dad about Chuck Axelrod wanting to tell the story of Buck McHenry on tonight's *Sportsline* show. Even though Mr. Henry didn't want anyone to know.

"Well," Dad said, "at least you don't have to worry about that now."

"My grampa's probably at the park, Jason," Aaron said.

It was already after four.

"You better go there, Aaron, and tell him what happened," Dad said. "Kim, you ought to call your father right now and tell him to contact his camera crew. I'm sure they have a phone in their truck. Jason, why don't you show Aaron where the park is? I'll walk Kim over after she's talked to her dad."

Aaron rose to go. I didn't feel like going any-where.

"Jason," Dad said, "the world's not coming to an end because you didn't recruit a baseball team."

"It's not just that, Dad," I said. "It's other stuff too. It's the story of Buck McHenry. People ought to know about him and now it won't get out. And the stories of those other great players too. People don't know about them either. They don't know how good those guys were and how they never had a chance to play in the big leagues because of the color of their skin. It was so unfair. Those guys were great ballplayers. Josh Gibson hit a home run out of Yankee Stadium. Babe Ruth never did that. John Henry Lloyd. Honus Wagner said he was the best player who ever lived. People don't know about Josh Gibson and John Henry Lloyd and Buck McHenry and Cool Papa Bell. They don't know about the kind of life those guys led. Mr. Henry said that half the time they never got paid. They never had coaching. They never had spring training. They just got out their gloves and played ball. They made do with what they had, Mr. Henry said. They were always making something out of nothing. They were great and no one knows

137

about them and now no one will." I felt like crying.

"That's good," Kim Axelrod said.

"What's good?" What a dumb thing to say that was.

"What you just said. Making something out of nothing."

"I didn't say that. Mr. Henry said that."

"My dad could do that too."

"Do what?"

"Make something out of nothing."

"What are you talking about?"

"It could be part of the story."

"Part of what story? There is no story. There's no team, there's no story, there's nothing."

"Jason, the storyline could be we don't have enough players for Buck McHenry to coach. So we advertise for players on Dad's show."

"That's crazy."

"Why's it crazy? There's got to be kids around who didn't play on any team last year who no one knows about. Kids that maybe don't even know there's an eleven-year-old league. New kids."

"There are no new kids."

"Aaron and I are new."

"You're probably the only new eleven-year-old kids in town."

"Probably is probably. You don't *know* that."

"This isn't Detroit. This is a small town."

"What's the population of Arborville?"

"A hundred thousand. Maybe a little more."

"Let's get the little more," Aaron said.

"You're as nuts as she is."

"Listen, kids," Dad said quietly, "you ought to stop arguing and go over to the park and let Mr. Henry know what's going on. And maybe, just maybe, there'll be some eleven-year-old kids playing there who might want to be on a team."

"Dad, by this time every eleven-year-old kid in Arborville who wants to be on a team is on one. I guarantee it."

Kim stood up. "You coming, Aaron?"

"Yeah."

"Aren't you going to call your dad?" I said.

"Nope. Let the camera crew come. Where's the park?"

"I like your spirit, Kim," Mom said. "Come. I'll show you where the park is."

"*I'll* show her, Mom. And please don't you and Dad come. This is going to be really embarrassing. A camera crew coming in from Detroit to shoot a three-man team."

"A three-*person* team," Kim said.

And now that too, I thought. Girls! Who needed them?

"Aaron needs a glove," she said.

"What for? We're not going to have a practice."

"You don't know what's going to happen, Jason. Do you have an extra glove?"

"Yes."

We went to the front hall and I opened the athletic box next to the closet and dug through old tennis balls, Frisbees, hockey pucks, and broken badminton rackets and found my old fielder's glove.

"It's pretty old."

"It's okay," Aaron said. "You got a ball?"

I looked at him. The memory of the fastball he threw at me in his backyard came back to me. "Here's a ball. You guys start walking. Go left. I'll catch up with you."

"Where're you going?" Kim asked.

"To get some sponges."

I ran back in the kitchen.

"Now what?" Dad said.

"Sponges for my catcher's mitt. Aaron throws hard." I looked under the sink.

"I like your new friends, Jason," Dad said.

"I like Aaron but she's not my friend."

"That's too bad because I think she's great," Mom said. "She's a super kid."

"She's spoiled. That signed Mickey Mantle

card. Her Dad being big TV sports show business."

"You're just jealous," Mom said.

"Of her? Not in a million years. She's probably a lousy ballplayer, and if we had a team we'd have to carry her just because her dad is the great Chuck Axelrod and also director of the eleven-year-old league." I stuffed two old sponges into my pocket. "See ya."

"Behave yourself," Dad said. Practically what Mrs. Henry said to Aaron before he and I took off from their house on our bikes.

I caught up with Aaron and Kim at the corner of Ferdon and Granger.

"We were just talking about your folks," she said. "They're really nice."

"They're all right."

She shook her head. "No, they're nice, Jason. I can tell. Most kids I know have all kinds of problems with their parents." She turned to Aaron. "How about you, Aaron?"

Bango. Out of nowhere. Here we are walking in sunlight to the park and she drops a bomb.

Aaron didn't answer right away. I shot her a warning look. She misread it.

"Are your folks divorced too?" she asked.

From bad to worse. Usually I'm terrific at

changing subjects. But this time I couldn't think of a thing to say.

"My folks got killed in a car crash," Aaron said quietly. "With my brother Louis."

Now are you happy, I thought. Now look what you've done.

She was shocked.

"I'm sorry," she said.

Aaron pounded the pocket of my old glove.

And then instead of cutting her losses and shutting up, she went on. She asked, "Were you in the crash?"

Was she out of her mind? Had she no sense at all?

Aaron shook his head. "I was home playing ball."

I couldn't stand it any longer. "The park's right there, past that senior citizens' shelter."

But it was like I didn't exist at all.

"Did your father coach your team?"

I could have throttled her.

"He coached my brother Louis's team when Louis was in Little League." Aaron suddenly grinned, remembering. "They were champs. Except Louis was going to be a football player. Always calling himself Mr. Q.B. He could throw a football a long way. He used to make me run and run and run and he could still throw it over my head. . . ."

I was stunned. Aaron was talking about his family and talking easily. He wasn't clamming up and looking the way he'd looked when I first met him. He was talking. About the tragedy.

Kim said, "Was your dad a professional ballplayer too?"

"He was a teacher. So was my mom."

"In the same school?"

"Yeah."

"Your school?"

"Yeah," Aaron laughed. "That's where they met. Before I was born though."

"That's like my folks," she said. "They met where they were working too. Only it was a TV studio. My mom did the weather. Dad did the sports. Where'd your folks meet, Jason?"

"I, uh . . ." I was tongue-tied. Confused by what had just happened. Her getting him to talk about stuff that used to shut him up. She'd somehow done what all the doctors in Tennessee hadn't been able to do, get Aaron to open up about his family. As for her question about where my folks met, I didn't know the answer to that either. I'd never asked my folks where they'd met.

"I guess they met here in Arborville," I said lamely.

"Were you born in Arborville?"

"Yeah. Where were you born?" Let's get off me, I thought.

"In Nashville. Do you have brothers and sisters?"

"No. Do you?"

She shook her head. Aaron didn't say anything. He didn't have any either now, I thought. We must have all thought that, because a silence suddenly descended on the three of us.

But it wasn't a bad silence. It was the kind of silence that happens when everyone's thinking the same thing and you don't *have* to talk.

We walked inside that silence together, the three of us, the rest of the way to the park.

14

Some parks are better than others. Sampson Park is a park for everyone, from little kids on jungle gyms to senior citizens playing cards. In between are parents and kids flying kites, dogs chasing sticks, tennis matches, baseball games, soccer games, kids riding bikes, college kids playing basketball or throwing Frisbees. It's a great big park for everyone.

It was fun seeing it through Kim's and Aaron's eyes as they saw it for the first time.

"Neat," Kim said, her eyes shining.

"It's nice," Aaron said softly.

I felt good. There are kids who come to Sampson Park and wonder what's so special about it. It's just another city park, they say. But it isn't. And Kim and Aaron felt that immediately.

"You see your grampa?" I asked.

"That's his truck. The yellow pickup. There he is."

"Where?"

"Leaning against the backstop."

Sure enough there was Mr. Henry, fingers in the metal mesh of the backstop, watching some college kids playing slow-pitch softball on diamond one, next to the parking lot.

"That's Buck McHenry?" Kim asked.

I guess she expected to see a baseball card picture, a ballplayer in a uniform. And all she was seeing was an old man in a fishing hat leaning against a backstop.

"You bet that's Buck McHenry," I said. "But remember, we don't call him that."

"Not even after my dad's *Sportsline* show when everybody knows?"

"*If* that comes off. Maybe then."

"Don't worry. It'll come off. If the crew gets here, Dad will use them. It costs too much not to."

It sounded like she knew a lot about the TV business.

"I wonder if we should tell him a crew is coming," I said.

"He could get mad," Aaron said.

"Better not tell him then."

"Hey, Grampa," Aaron yelled.

Mr. Henry turned around. It took him a second to see who was calling him, but when he did

146

he smiled and waved to us to come down to the diamond.

Aaron started running slowly. I turned to Kim. "Let's see how good of a runner you are."

She didn't need to be asked twice. She took off like a shot. She passed Aaron like he was standing still. When I got there, she was looking up at Mr. Henry and he was looking down at her, amused.

"You got fine runnin' legs, girl," he was saying. He turned to Aaron. "You been behavin' yourself, boy?"

"Yeah, Grampa."

"That's good." He looked at me. "Where's the rest of our team, Jason?"

Here we go, I thought. "There is no rest of the team, Mr. Henry."

Mr. Henry pursed his lips in a silent surprised whistle.

"We couldn't get any of the kids on the list to come," I explained.

"What do you know about that?" He didn't sound too disappointed.

On the other side of the backstop the softball game was ending. The players were shaking hands.

"Well, we can't have us a team with only three players," Mr. Henry said cheerfully.

"My dad'll recruit players, Coach," Kim said. And the word "coach" crackled in the air.

Mr. Henry smiled at Kim. "How's your daddy goin' to recruit players, young lady?"

"He has a TV show."

"I know about that. But they don't make ballplayers on Channel 4, do they?"

"He could advertise on the show for eleven-year-old ballplayers."

"Advertise?" Mr. Henry laughed.

"He could. My dad can do just about anything. Here he comes now. We can ask him."

We looked where she was looking. A white Lincoln Continental had pulled into the parking lot. Inside it, Chuck Axelrod was still on the phone.

He pulled the Lincoln up to the edge of the parking lot, only a few yards from where we were standing. He popped the trunk.

"Grab the bag, kids," he called out the window and then went on talking on the phone. We could hear him clearly.

"Tony, you're only about a mile from the State Road exit. Take that exit. Make a right turn and all you've got to do is follow State Road into town. You'll go past a golf course, under a bridge. You'll see a street called Granger on your right. Take it and follow it to . . ."

He was talking to the film unit who were on I-94. They were almost in town. I got a shaky sensation in my stomach. I looked at Mr. Henry. He was watching Chuck Axelrod, fascinated. He had no idea what was coming down the Interstate toward him.

Aaron and Kim hauled an equipment bag that had ARBORVILLE REC LEAGUES stenciled on it out of the Lincoln's trunk.

"Imagine that," Mr. Henry murmured. "Chuck Axelrod himself, delivering me bats and balls."

Chuck Axelrod hung up his phone, jumped out of the Lincoln, and came running up to Mr. Henry, his right hand pumping in front of him.

"Chuck Axelrod," he said.

Mr. Henry shook his hand and smiled. "Now you don't have to tell me that. I see you on TV all the time."

Chuck Axelrod laughed. "Well, I've heard a lot about you too, Mr. Buck McHenry."

And there it was again. The secret that wouldn't stay a secret. Mr. Henry's face didn't change expression. Maybe he hadn't heard it and maybe Chuck Axelrod wouldn't repeat it.

Kim and Aaron were taking stuff out of the bag. They took out a pair of shin guards, a chest protector, four bats, a catcher's mask, and five new baseballs. What did they think was going to happen anyway?

Chuck Axelrod said, "When the kids told me that the great Buck McHenry was living right here in Arborville, I couldn't believe it."

Mr. Henry heard that, all right. He gave me a sorrowful look.

"The boys have lent me your baseball card, Mr. McHenry," Chuck Axelrod went on. He had it out and was looking at the stats side. "It says you're working in town here as a school custodian."

It didn't say that at all. I'd said that. All the card said was that he was a school janitor in Michigan.

"I don't know why you quit at the height of your career. But I figure that's something we can bring out on the show."

Mr. Henry cleared his throat. "I'm afraid there's been a mistake here, Mr. Axelrod." He sounded worried. Scrapes with the law were coming back to haunt him. And it was all my fault.

"Oh, there's been no mistake, Buck. I know you've taken another name. But that's all part of the story. You know what I like best about it, Buck? What I like best is that it's not just going to be about the past but about the present and the future. I mean, sir, here you are. Come out of a self-imposed obscurity, anonymity, if you will, to coach a kids' baseball team. And not just any kids' team but a team made up of rejects. Rejects the way fifty years ago you and your teammates were rejected from baseball. Do you see it, Buck? That's how we'll start. Interview you, show you coaching your team . . ."

As Chuck Axelrod went on outlining the TV show, he began steering Mr. Henry toward the diamond. A powerful little tugboat pushing a big old ocean liner out to sea. The big old ocean liner was helpless.

I went over to Kim. "Listen," I whispered, "please tell your dad there's no story. Tell him no more kids are coming. Tell him there's no team."

"It won't make any difference, Jason. My dad'll get us a team." She was pounding the pocket of her glove with one of the new baseballs.

"You worried about my grampa being mad 'cause of the secret?" Aaron asked.

I couldn't very well tell Aaron I was worried about what those scrapes with the law had been. For all I knew, Mr. Henry was still a fugitive from the law.

"Grampa's goin' to be okay, Jason. He's going

to get used to being Buck McHenry again."

Chuck Axelrod must have run out of breath for a second because now Mr. Henry was talking. "I watch your *Sportsline* show every Saturday night, Mr. Axelrod. I like it. But I can't be on it."

"Yes, you can, Grampa," Aaron cried out.

Mr. Henry wouldn't look at him. "First of all, there isn't even going to be a team for me to coach. The kids haven't told you that, have they?"

"What do you mean there isn't going to be a team for you to coach?" Chuck Axelrod looked over at us.

"We couldn't get any of the kids on the list to come out for the team," Kim said. "But I thought you could advertise on the show for players. Couldn't that be part of the storyline?"

For the first time in his life, I think, Chuck Axelrod was at loss for words.

"Couldn't you advertise for players for us, Dad?"

"I don't believe this, Kim. Are you saying you couldn't recruit *any* kids?"

She nodded.

"When you called them, didn't you tell them Buck McHenry was going to coach them?"

"No."

"Why not?"

"Jason said it was supposed to be a secret."

"That's right," Mr. Henry said firmly. "And it's got to stay a secret."

"A secret?" Chuck Axelrod laughed half hysterically. "I've got a camera crew coming in from Detroit and you're telling me it's all supposed to be a secret. Why in heaven's name would you want it to be a secret anyway? Here you are, the legendary Buck McHenry, coming out of a self-imposed anonymity to coach a bunch of kids—why in heaven's name should that be a secret? Why, we ought to holler the news from the rooftops. It should be broadcast to every corner of the land. It would be an inspiration to every American."

It was like he was on TV right now. I felt like clapping.

Then I looked at Mr. Henry and his face was tight and anxious.

"Mr. Henry," I said, "can I say something?"

He didn't even look at me. He didn't trust me anymore. I didn't blame him.

"Those scrapes with the law, Mr. Henry. I just know they couldn't mean anything after all these years."

Chuck Axelrod held up the baseball card. "I saw that too. Is that why you don't want the world to know about you, sir? Because you didn't pay a parking ticket thirty years ago?"

Mr. Henry looked trapped.

"Buck, whatever it was, it's ancient history now. Secondly, who hasn't made mistakes in their youth? But all that's long ago. As the boy said, it's dead material. What remains is alive and immortal."

Chuck Axelrod was really flying now. But Mr. Henry wasn't listening. "Get your bike, Aaron. We're going home."

"Listen, Buck, if you're worried about not having a team to coach, you can stop worrying now. Kim's right. I can get you kids. And that *will* be the storyline. Thanks, honey. What do you say, Buck? Do we let the world know?"

"Mr. Axelrod, my name is not Buck McHenry. It's Mack Henry. It has been Mack Henry for a long, long time. Folks are confused enough these days. I don't want to confuse them any more. Where's your bike, boy?"

"At Jason's house," Aaron said reluctantly.

"We'll go get it and put it in the truck."

He started to walk off. Chuck Axelrod jumped in front of him. Mr. Henry looked old and tall and dignified and puzzled.

Chuck Axelrod grinned. "If you're worried about confusing people, Buck, let me tell you something. I've been in the media business a long time. And when TV wants to, it can uncon- fuse people faster than it can confuse them. Es- pecially when they're presented with the truth. And that's what we are after. The truth. Listen to this storyline. That's all I ask you, sir. Listen to the storyline. . . ."

Chuck Axelrod went into a crouch as he talked. A storyteller's crouch.

"Buck McHenry comes out of the past to coach a team fighting to be born. But what happens? Only three kids show up. Will the team die before it was born? Only some eleven-year-old viewers in Arborville, Michigan, can write a happy end for this story. So if anyone out there is eleven years old, living in Arborville, and is not already on a baseball team, Buck McHenry needs you. Call him at, and we give them your phone num- ber. What do you say? Is it a winner or isn't it? Do you like it?"

"Yes," I said.

"Yes," Kim said.

"Yes," Aaron said.

Mr. Henry shook his head. He was smiling faintly. "I admire your talent, sir. I surely do. But no youngsters showing up here today, I think that's God's way of sending us a message. And that message is we better not have a team this year. So my grandson and me are goin' home. Get in the truck, boy. We're going over to Jason's house to get your bicycle."

"Please, Grampa," Aaron begged. "Let him do the show."

"Boy," Mr. Henry said, anger coming into his voice, "I am going home. You coming with me or not?"

"But you said you'd coach us, Grampa."

"There's no one to coach, boy. There aren't even enough bodies for a practice."

"Wait a second," Chuck Axelrod said. "What do you mean there's not enough bodies? I'm a body. You're a body. That makes five of us already. And—" He looked around the park. And then he started to laugh. "Talk about messages from God. We're receiving one now. Do you all see what I see? A bunch of kids with baseball gloves coming toward us? Tell me those kids are not looking for a little action, Buck. I defy you to tell me that."

Coming across the park on bicycles were kids our age. "I bet my bottom dollar those kids are looking for a team to join," Chuck Axelrod said.

Considering Chuck Axelrod's income as a big TV sportscaster, Mr. Henry and I could have made a lot of money right then and there. We were the only ones there who knew those kids weren't looking for a team to join. They were already on one. My old team. Baer Machine.

There was Cal Borker and Art Silver and Diaz and Tug Murphy and Kevin Kovich and Tim Corrigan and Greg Conklin and a couple of others. They must have heard about our team meeting and had come down to laugh at us. And that, I thought, was just about the last thing we needed.

I ran out to ask them to go away.

"What're you guys doing here?"

"That's a nice greeting, Jayce," Pete said. "Here we been looking all over town for you and you ask what we're doing here. What're *you* doing here? What's Mr. Henry doing here?"

And then they all started peppering me at once.

"Is that your new team?"

"You're short a few players."

"Who's the girl?"

"Who's the black kid?"

"What's the deal on Mr. Henry?"

"Is the girl on your team?"

"She's pretty but can she hit for power?"

"Hey, that looks like Chuck Axelrod."

"No, it don't."

"Sure, it's him."

"He looks fatter on TV."

"He *is* fatter on TV."

"What's he doing here, Jason?"

"Come on, Jason, what's going on?"

"All right, if I tell you guys what's going on, will you all leave then?"

"Jason sounds like he's ashamed of us."

"I don't blame him. I'm ashamed of us too."

"It's a free country."

"I'm serious. If I tell you, will you leave?"

"Maybe," Tim said.

I'd have to settle for "maybe." "Okay. The Grandstand's going to sponsor my new team. Chuck Axelrod is helping us organize it. The girl is his daughter. The boy is Mr. Henry's grandson. And Mr. Henry is going to coach our team."

"Mr. Henry?" Diaz broke up. "What's he know about baseball?"

"A lot more than you ever will, Pete," I shot back. The idea of Pete Diaz sneering at a baseball legend like Buck McHenry was too much for me. "It just so happens Mr. Henry played in the old Negro leagues. His name was Buck McHenry then and he was a big star. I've even got a baseball card of him."

They looked at me as though I was nuts. Then Tim Corrigan started laughing. "Mr. Henry on a baseball card? Jayce, you just collected one card too many."

That broke them up.

"Okay, I told you guys what was going on. Why don't you go now?"

"We want to meet Chuck Axelrod."

"He doesn't want to meet you guys."

"If he doesn't want to meet us, how come he's yelling for us to come over?" Greg Conklin said quietly.

I looked back toward the diamond. Chuck Axelrod had made a megaphone of his hands and was shouting, "Jason, bring those kids over here."

"That's it. We are being summoned," Kovich said.

"Maybe he wants to put us on television," Pete said. "How's my hair look?"

"Ugly."

"Let's go," Cal said.

"Last one there's in love with Chuck Axelrod's daughter," Art said.

They raced their bikes to the diamond. I ran after them. By the time I got there the air was filled with greetings to Mr. Henry. "Hi, Mr. Henry. How ya doin', Mr. Henry? How's it going, Mr. Henry?" All the while they were looking out of the corners of their eyes at Chuck Axelrod.

Chuck Axelrod knew what was going on, all right. He had to be used to people looking at him on the sly. Meanwhile Mr. Henry answered their greetings.

"Hello, Pete. Calvin. Kevin. Greg. Tug, Art, Jim."

Often the only people in a school who know all the kids' names are the principal and the custodian. And the custodian always knows them first. Starting with the kids who mess up the lunchroom.

"I guess you know these boys, Buck," Chuck Axelrod said, his eyes gleaming.

I wondered if the guys had heard that "Buck." I couldn't tell.

"I guess I know some of them since they were in kindergarten."

"I get it. You're the custodian in *their* school?"

"You've got it right, sir."

"Love it, love it." Chuck Axelrod took out his pad and started making notes. He paused. "How old are you kids?"

"We're eleven," Diaz said.

"Eleven and a half," Greg Conklin said.

"You're eleven like the rest of us, Conklin."

"I'm gonna be twelve in July," Kovich said.

"Kovich got left back."

"Hold it," Chuck Axelrod said. "All I'm trying to find out is if you're eligible to play in the eleven-year-old league."

"Yes," they all said.

"Good. Then I've got a proposition for you. How'd you like to join a brand-new team coached by one of the greatest right-handed pitchers of all time—Mr. Buck McHenry."

With a sweeping gesture, like a circus ringmaster, Chuck Axelrod pointed to Mr. Henry.

The guys were stunned. They hadn't believed me when I told them that, but now it was the voice of Channel 4 sports talking. That made it true.

Mr. Henry looked as though he'd just been shot.

"Mr. Henry," Pete said humbly, "is it true what Jason told us, that you're on a baseball card?"

This was worth everything.

"He sure is, son," Chuck Axelrod said and whipped out the Buck McHenry card. "I've got it right here. Mr. McHenry is too modest. He won't blow his own horn but by God I'll blow it for him." He held the card up. They crowded around.

"Don't push, Borker."

"I can't see it."

"Is that really you, Mr. Henry?"

"It don't look like him."

"It's an old picture, man."

"When was it taken, Mr. Henry?"

"Who'd you play for?"

"How come you never told anyone?"

"I bet my dad heard about you."

"It says on the back who he played for."

"It says he became a school custodian."

"Where?"

"In Michigan, jerk."

"I mean, where on the card?"

"There."

"Don't bend it, Kovich. You're goin' to tear it."

"Does it say Eberwoods?"

"Quit shovin', Corrigan."

"Take it easy, guys," Chuck Axelrod said, laughing. I looked at the others. Aaron was so proud. Kim was smiling. But Mr. Henry stood silent as a statue.

We're getting him into trouble, I thought. I felt so guilty.

"Easy now, this card has to stay in good shape," Chuck Axelrod was saying. "I've got to take pictures of it. Let's have it back. Here we go. Thank you, gentlemen, thank you."

He put the card in his shirt pocket. "Kids, my name's Chuck Axelrod, and I do sports for Channel 4."

They all laughed.

"We know *that*."

"We watch your *Sportsline* show all the time, Mr. Axelrod."

"It's my favorite show on the air."

"Mine too."

"Good. Then how would you all like to be on tonight's show?"

That really stopped them. And no one more so than Pete Diaz, for all his jokes about being on TV. "What'd I tell you guys?" he said, and began nervously patting his hair.

"What do we got to do?" Tug asked.

"Join this new team—The Grandstand."

Silence. They looked at each other. I spoke up for them.

"They're already on a team, Mr. Axelrod. My old team—Baer Machine."

Chuck Axelrod looked at me reproachfully. "Thanks a lot, Jason. You could have warned me."

"How could he have, Dad?" Kim said. "He couldn't have got a word in edgewise."

She was defending me!

Chuck Axelrod laughed. "Honey, you're absolutely right. I'm a victim of my own scenario. I just wanted something to happen real bad. But . . ." He turned to the rest of us. "You know what I always say?"

No one had the slightest idea what he always said.

"I always say, if you can't join 'em, beat 'em."

It was the opposite of what you're supposed to say, but no one laughed because we couldn't tell if he had mixed up the language or meant it.

It turned out he meant it.

"Here's what I propose. I've got a camera crew coming in from Detroit. They should be here any minute to shoot a feature story on Buck McHenry for tonight's show. I'm going to need game action to run copy over. I want to have Mr. McHenry coaching in a game situation. So here's the plan. A three-inning practice game between Baer Machine and The Grandstand. What do you say?"

"They've only got three players, Mr. Axelrod," Art said.

"We can beat you with three players," Kim snapped.

I hoped she played as tough as she talked.

"And just how are you going to beat us with three players?" Kevin asked her.

"Aaron can pitch, Jason can catch—"

"That's a matter of opinion," Pete cracked.

She ignored him. "—and I can play the field."

165

Chuck Axelrod grinned at Mr. Henry. "How do you like your team's spirit, Coach?"

Mr. Henry, who hadn't said a word since being introduced as Buck McHenry, was silent. I could tell that he still wanted out.

"What do you say, Coach?" Chuck Axelrod repeated.

Mr. Henry sighed. "I admire your daughter's spirit, sir. But I've got to agree with my boys from Eberwoods School. Nine against three can't be a ball game. So I guess we better all shake hands and go home. Let's go, Aaron."

Chuck Axelrod laughed. "Buck, it's a darn good thing you don't have to produce a TV show every week. You give up too easy. Kim, you remember a segment we did last year with Fast Eddie Phipps?"

"Sure. My dad did a show with a fast-pitch softball team that had only three players on it."

"Fast Eddie Phipps, king of the fast-pitch softball pitchers," Chuck Axelrod said. "And all he had on his team was a pitcher, catcher, and first baseman."

"I saw that!" Pete said, excited. "He didn't even need the first baseman. He was unhittable."

"Well, Aaron's unhittable too," I said, nodding in Aaron's direction. They all looked at him.

"You a pitcher?" Cal asked.

"I pitch some."

Just the way he said that, so modestly, you could see they were impressed.

"You eleven?" Kevin asked. I knew they probably thought he was older. He was so big and strong-looking.

"I'm eleven," Aaron said shyly.

The real leader of the Baer Machine team was Tug Murphy. He was quiet. He led by example. Right now I watched Tug making up his mind. I could tell that he wanted to bat against Aaron. Tug was a jock; Aaron was a jock. You could see jock juices flowing back and forth between them.

"I'm willing to play them a three-inning practice game," Tug said quietly.

That settled it. "Me too," Pete said. "Anything to be on TV."

"Sure. Okay. Let's do it," they chorused.

"Good. The game will start in fifteen minutes," Chuck Axelrod said.

"What about the camera crew?" Pete, of course, asked.

"They're here now," Chuck Axelrod said. "I'll be right back."

None of us had seen it arrive—a large white van with a tall antenna on top and the words

WVID-TV, DETROIT on the side. It was parked not far from Chuck Axelrod's Lincoln.

"You believe this?" Kovich said, awed as we watched two men come out of the van. One carried a camera and wore a fat belt around his waist. The other carried what looked like a recorder and a pole with a microphone.

Chuck Axelrod was talking to them and pointing toward us.

"Unreal," Diaz said.

"Wait till I tell my folks," Kevin said. I think all our hearts were beating faster. We were going to be on TV. We were going to be famous.

Only Mr. Henry didn't look happy. Aaron saw it too and went up to him. "It's okay, isn't it, Grampa?" He was pleading with him.

Mr. Henry was silent. He didn't even look at Aaron.

"We're just going to play three innings, Grampa. That's all. Just three innings."

Mr. Henry looked down at his grandson. And then he smiled. A funny sad little smile. "What's got to be has got to be, I guess," he said.

He turned and looked at the Baer Machine guys, who were watching the camera crew haul more gear out of their truck.

"Haven't you boys ever seen a movie camera before? You aiming to be ballplayers or movie stars? Don't you know you can hurt your arm in a three-inning game just as bad as in a regular one? Start loosening up those muscles. Start warming up."

I could have clapped my hands. He was going to take a chance. He was staying. He was coaching!

I grabbed one of the new baseballs. "Aaron, let's warm up. Throw easy. Save your arm and we'll save a few surprises for them."

Mr. Henry chuckled. "Now you're talking, boy. Talking like a real catcher. Like Campy, Gibson, Radcliffe, any of them."

It gave me goose pimples to hear that. It was the greatest compliment any kid could've got. Please, dear God, I prayed, don't let me mess up.

Kim warmed up off to one side with Mr. Henry. I didn't really get a chance to check out how she looked. I was busy warming up Aaron. He threw easy. Saving the surprises for later.

16

Well, the game or the TV show, or whatever you want to call what happened next, started out just fine.

The man with the camera and fat belt—which Kim told me was the battery pack for the camera—was tied by a cable to the man with a recorder and a microphone. The moment they got to the diamond, they set up a little black-and-white TV monitor so we could see ourselves.

Then the cameraman said, "Rolling, Chuck," and after a few seconds the man with the video recorder said, "Speed," and then without warning Chuck Axelrod began interviewing Mr. Henry. This was how it went:

CHUCK AXELROD: Mr. McHenry, you came out of a self-imposed obscurity to coach a kids' baseball team. Could you tell us why?

MR. HENRY (*fiddling with his fisherman's hat*): My grandson moved to Michigan from Tennessee. He was looking for a team to play on up here. And there was a new team looking for a coach. We were starting together. Me and my grandson.

CHUCK AXELROD: Let's have the grandson over here. C'mere, son. What's your name?

AARON (*so quiet you almost didn't hear him*): Aaron.

CHUCK AXELROD: All right, Aaron. Crowd right in. The golden rule of television is when you feel uncomfortable is when you look good. Now, Aaron, speak up and tell the folks at home what it feels like to have your grampa, one of the great ballplayers of all time, coaching your team.

AARON (*grinning, speaking a little louder*): Feels good.

CHUCK AXELROD (*laughing*): I bet it does. Was it your idea?

AARON: No, sir. It was Jason who started it. He found out who my grampa was. I didn't even know who my grampa was, did I, Grampa?

MR. HENRY (*smiling that funny little smile*): No, boy, I guess you didn't.

CHUCK AXELROD: Let's get Jason in here too then. The more the merrier.

He said that as though it was spontaneous, but I could tell he had planned it. I walked into the group and faced the camera with them.

CHUCK AXELROD: Folks, this is Jason Ross. Jason, how about telling our viewers just how you found Buck McHenry?

ME: Well, it started with me being cut. . . .

And then I told the whole story. About being cut from Baer Machine, finding out there was going to be an expansion team, returning the bases to Eberwoods School, Mr. Henry coaching me in the corridor, him pitching the invisible ball. Out of the corner of my eye I saw the Baer Machine guys listening fascinated. They didn't know any of what had happened after I left them. And then I told how I discovered the Buck McHenry baseball card at The Grandstand. Jim would love the plug. And then how I went to Mr. Henry's house, met Aaron, how Mr. Henry finally admitted he was Buck McHenry, and then how Aaron and I met up with Kim Axelrod, but we weren't able to recruit any other players— not even rejects from other teams—so here we were at Sampson Park with a great coach but no team.

All this Chuck Axelrod let me say without interruption. When I was done, he turned to the camera and said, "So if there are any eleven-year-olds in the city of Arborville watching our show tonight who want to play on a baseball team, there's a team called The Grandstand, coached by a baseball immortal, looking for you. How do they get on your team, Buck?

MR. HENRY (*startled*): Uh, I guess they call me. Or Jason. Better call Jason. Because I'm appointing him captain right now.

ME (*promptly*): My phone number's 555-8742. They can call me there. Can we start our game now, Mr. Henry?

CHUCK AXELROD: Say that number again, Jason. You never say important things only once on TV.

ME: 555-8742. Can we—?

CHUCK AXELROD: Hang on a second more, Jason. Folks, you just heard Jason here call Buck McHenry "Mr. Henry." Well, therein lies perhaps the most interesting part of tonight's *Sportsline* feature story.

Oh no, I thought. Here it comes. Be nice, Mr. Axelrod. Be kind to Mr. Henry, I prayed.

CHUCK AXELROD (*holding up the Buck McHenry baseball card*): This is the baseball card Jason just mentioned. Can we get a close-up of it? There it is. Now on the back of this Negro League baseball star card, it says . . .

I didn't dare look at Mr. Henry. His scrapes with the law were about to be on TV.

Sure enough, Chuck Axelrod read the part about Buck McHenry quitting baseball and becoming a school custodian in Michigan. And he told the whole world how Buck McHenry had changed his name by dividing it in half, McHenry becoming Mack Henry.

And then he turned to Mr. Henry—I was watching this on the television monitor.

CHUCK AXELROD: Could you tell our viewers why the great Buck McHenry, at the height of his baseball career, quit the sport to become a school custodian in Michigan?

At that moment I was so scared for Mr. Henry. I looked at his face on the monitor. It was without expression. Was he panicking inside? The silence was deafening. And then Chuck Axelrod, like one of those birds of prey that dive into the ocean after a fish, dove in after Mr. Henry.

CHUCK AXELROD: On the back of the card, Buck, it says you dropped out because of, and I quote, "scrapes with the law." Would you like to comment on that? Or . . . (*he smiled*) perhaps you wouldn't.

Mr. Henry stood there with everyone looking at him. Me, Aaron, Kim, Chuck Axelrod, the Baer Machine kids, the cameraman, the recorder man, and through those guys—the whole world. Mr. Henry stood there alone and helpless.

"It's okay, Grampa," I heard Aaron whisper.

174

More silence. Then Mr. Henry gave a strange little laugh. "My grandson says it's okay. So I guess it's got to be. You were asking, sir, about those scrapes with the law?"

"Yes, sir," Chuck Axelrod said.

"Well, I didn't kill anyone, if that's what you're after. Or rob anyone either."

He looked past Chuck Axelrod, past the camera crew, past the kids, past, it even seemed to me, Sampson Park. He was looking into years gone by.

"Those scrapes with the law had to do with how us colored ballplayers were treated in the old days. In those days when the season was over, some of us used to go barnstormin' around the country. You know, go from country town to country town playin' the local team. Some of those local boys would be all right ballplayers but most were just strong farm boys. Their fans would pay a dollar to see the local heroes lick a team of traveling professional black baseball players. And if they licked us, we'd get half of each dollar.

"Of course they couldn't have really licked us in a month of Sundays, but if we wanted to get paid, well, we had to let them lick us."

"You mean you threw ball games?" Chuck Axelrod asked. "You lost them on purpose?"

"You could say that, Mr. Axelrod. You could also say we earned our pay, because it was a lot harder to lose to those teams than it was to beat them. And one particular night, as I recall, it was especially hard. One night we didn't lose when we were supposed to. The reason was their fans got down on us pretty good, hollering all sorts of nasty stuff. Racial things, you know. I was supposed to walk a few batters and let the rest hit easy pitches. Anyway, they're hollerin' at me that my daddy had been swinging in a tree in Africa with the rest of the apes and what was I doing playing an American sport. There was so much of that that I got mad, and before I knew it, I started firing my smoker. Well, those white boys had never seen anything like that. They never lifted the bat off their shoulders. Up they came and down they went. My teammates got mad too because of all the nasty name-calling and when they came up to bat, instead of striking out and falling down and looking like clowns like we were bein' paid to do, they began hitting the hide off the ball. Home runs, triples, doubles, and racin' round those bases like we were shot out of cannons. Before you knew it we were fifteen runs up on a team we were supposed to lose to."

Mr. Henry chuckled. "Well, sir, to make a long story short, we won the game but not the war. The boys asked me to ask the promoter if we could at least have expense money to get out of town. We didn't want the hundred dollars they were supposed to pay us. We just wanted enough money to buy gas. The promoter said to me, 'Boy, you're going to be lucky to git out of here in one piece. Git, now, git.' Like he was talkin' to a dog.

"The gate receipts were sittin' on his desk. Maybe a thousand dollars. I grabbed four dollars. Four dollars. That'd buy us enough gas to get us out of town. I grabbed the four dollars and I ran. The promoter came around the desk after me shouting, 'Stop that nigger,' and worse, and pretty soon there were sheriff's deputies and folks with guns coming after me. I jumped into one of my teammate's cars. In those days we traveled in two old cars, and by the time we ran out of gas, we had air conditioning through those cars. We were lucky they thought they'd killed us all and didn't come out to bury our bodies."

He laughed. No one else did.

"That was only one time. But there were other experiences like that. Well, a man can only take so much, you know. I couldn't take it anymore, so I got out. I think the hardest thing in life is to listen to folks call you a lot of names and not be able to hit back. And maybe even worse than that, from a ballplayer's point of view, is to lose to teams you know you can beat with one hand tied behind your back. I told myself there's got to be easier ways of making money. And I found one. I found out that pushing a broom was a lot easier than pitching a ball game, taking abuse, and losing on purpose." He looked Chuck Axelrod straight in the eye. "You ask about my scrapes with the law. And now I told you."

With that he was silent. Everyone was silent. My eyes felt moist. I looked around. Kim's eyes were wet too. Kovich and Diaz had tears in their eyes. The camera kept on shooting us; the recorder kept on recording.

Chuck Axelrod broke the silence. "The past is dead. Today, Buck McHenry is back in baseball. This time as the coach of his grandson's team. Coach McHenry, can you get your team on the field?"

Mr. Henry clapped his hands. "Jason, you're catching. Get your gear on, boy. Aaron, you're pitching. Young lady, you're going to have to play everywhere else. You just play each batter where I tell you to."

Then, while I was putting on my catcher's gear, Mr. Henry did a classy thing. He walked over to the Baer Machine kids. "Calvin, Tim, Tug, seeing as how you don't have yourselves a coach, how'd you like me to coach your team too?"

He did that without consulting with Chuck Axelrod. That's what I mean by a classy move.

Tug said, "Thanks, Mr. Hen—McHenry, we'll keep the same lineup we had this morning."

"You mind if I root for your team too, boy?"

"That'd be great, Mr. McHenry," Pete said.

"Pete, the rest of you, you listen to me, my name's still Mr. Henry. The way it's always been. You forget about that McHenry stuff. Nothing's changed. Tug, get your batting order set. You boys'll be first up seein' as this appears to be The Grandstand's home field."

Mr. Henry walked over to me. "No signals, Jason. Just let Aaron pitch how he wants."

"Yes, sir."

In the infield, Tug was throwing ground balls to Kim so she could warm up. She looked smooth scooping and throwing. She threw like a boy. Fielded like a boy. I wouldn't be a bit surprised if she didn't hit like a boy. I wouldn't also be a bit surprised if her baseball card collection was as good as she said it was.

"Jason, get your mind off baseball cards." I could hear Mr. Borker's voice inside my head. And he was right.

I squatted down. Aaron was doing some land-scaping around the mound. Kicking the dirt. Getting the feel of it. Every pitcher's mound is different.

I pounded my glove. My two sponges were in. I'd need them. He'd be throwing his smoker all the time. He'd have to. And throw it high, too, so if they did hit the ball, they'd pop it up to Kim or him. Ground balls and we were dead. We didn't have a first baseman. Strike-outs and pop-ups were what we wanted. And no fly balls. A fly ball was a home run.

While Aaron threw easy, Mr. Henry went out and positioned Kim to play between first and second. I knew he was figuring they'd be swing-ing late on Aaron's smoker. They were all right-handed hitters too.

The Baer Machine kids eyed Aaron as he warmed up. Even throwing easy, they could see from his motion, his kick, his stride, that he was a thrower. What they didn't know yet was how hard he could throw. Well, in a few seconds they'd find out.

"I'll call balls and strikes from behind the

mound," Chuck Axelrod announced. "You rolling, Tony?"

"You bet, ump," the cameraman said, laughing.

"Speed," called out the man with the recorder.

"Batter up," Chuck Axelrod shouted.

17

Kevin Kovich stepped in.

"No batter," I yelled.

"No stick," Kim yelled.

"Make him get one over, Kevin," Mr. Henry called out, coaching for them too. He was reminding Baer Machine that you should always take one with a new pitcher. See what he's got.

Well, it turned out Kevin didn't see a thing.

Aaron wound up, kicked, and fired, and it came just like the bullet he threw in his backyard. This time I stuck with it. The ball exploded in my mitt. And, despite the two sponges, my hand stung. "Ouch," I said.

"Strike one," Chuck Axelrod said.

"Holy cow," Kevin Kovich said.

"Choke up, Kevin," Mr. Henry called out. "Move back in the batter's box." And then he shouted to Aaron. "Keep firing, boy. Keep throwing trouble."

Aaron and I grinned at each other. "Trouble"

was Satchel Paige's pitch.

"Stan," Chuck Axelrod shouted at the man with the recorder, "are you picking up Mr. McHenry's voice? He's coaching both teams."

"I'm getting it, Chuck," the sound man called back. He was wearing earphones.

"Jayce, I didn't even see that ball," Kevin said to me.

"You won't see the next one either, Kev."

"I hope he breaks your hand," Kevin said. I noticed he choked up on his bat the way Mr. Henry suggested.

"Blow it by him again, Aaron," Kim called out, pounding her glove.

I nodded to Aaron, wiggled one finger just for the heck of it, and braced myself. Aaron pumped, kicked, and fired, and once more the ball exploded in my mitt and once more Chuck Axelrod yelled "strike" and once more Kevin hadn't swung.

I could feel for him. It's hard to swing at what you can't see. And Kevin just couldn't see it. Nor could Cal, who was up after him. Or Tug after Cal. Tug at least swung, but he didn't come close to connecting. I wished he had. I wished someone would hit a few fouls. It would give me a little break. My left hand was beginning to hurt.

183

Up they came and down they went. Aaron struck out one guy after another. In the next inning it was Tim, Pete, Art standing there with their bats on the shoulders. Not even one foul tip.

Kim yelled. I yelled—once in pain, though I masked it by shouting "wow" instead of "ouch."

Mr. Henry didn't yell. He kept talking quietly to the Baer Machine kids telling them to choke up, stand in the back of the batter's box, don't take a big swing, just make contact. They listened and did what he said, except for making contact. That was easier said than done.

I wondered what Chuck Axelrod was going to make of Mr. Henry coaching both teams. And coaching *them* more than us. After the first two guys went down on strikes, all he ever said to Aaron was, "Keep mailin' trouble, boy."

Kim picked it up. "Mail them trouble, Aaron babe. Be a postman, mail them trouble."

It was hard to believe a girl could pick up on stuff like that, but she did. And in our half of the first inning she put her money where her mouth was with the bat. She jumped on Cal's first pitch and hit it over Greg's head at second for a single. She was for real. Cal is one of the best pitchers in the eleven-year-old league, but she'd pinged him like she owned him. I batted second. When I stood in there, Cal said, "Well, I can get *you* out at least."

"Don't count on it," I said.

But I'm sorry to say he did get me out. I popped up to Tim at first. And that brought up Aaron. I don't think any of us had thought of who would bat next if Kim was still on base and Aaron made out. Could Kim come in and bat again? And me take her place on first? It *was* crazy having only three players.

I'd never seen Aaron hit. I expected Mr. Henry to shout encouragement down to Aaron, but he didn't. Instead he shouted encouragement to Cal. "Send trouble the other way, Calvin."

Tug called out, "Pitchers can't hit, Cal."

Maybe Cal thought differently, because he threw the first one in the dirt and the second one wide and the third one high. He was trying too hard.

"You're overthrowing, boy," Mr. Henry called out. "Just throw to Tug's glove. Don't worry about the batter."

"That's right," Tug called out. "This guy's no stick. He's all show."

"You got to drive Kim in, Aaron," I yelled. "She's up next."

I was trying to tell him to hit the 3 and 0

cripple. It wouldn't do just to hit a single or take a walk. He really had to whack it, and a 3 and 0 pitch is the one to whack.

Aaron nodded. He looked relaxed up there in an open stance, feet apart.

Cal went to a full motion. Kim took off on it and Cal threw a fat one down the middle. Aaron stepped into it and drove it. Oh my, how he drove it! Swinging hips, shoulders, arms, and wrists, he drove it on a line starting low and rising higher and higher like a cannonball.

The prettiest sound in the world is when a bat makes solid on-the-nose contact with a ball. And the prettiest sight in the world is to see that ball keep going off, rising and rising.

In center field, Diaz didn't even move. He stood there and watched the ball shoot over his head like a rocket. It touched down way beyond him, near where some little kids were flying kites. The kids looked around. Where did *that* come from?

By the time Pete got to it, Aaron was back on the bench, not even breathing hard. Kim slapped him five. "Man, you hit that a ton," she said.

"Didn't he ever?" I said, and slapped him and her.

Mr. Henry came up behind Aaron and rubbed

his head. "I guess you did play some in Tennessee, boy."

"I got lucky, Grampa," Aaron said.

"You sure did," Mr. Henry chuckled proudly.

Kim and I laughed. We were a small team, three players and a coach, but we were a team.

Out on the mound, Cal Borker kicked angrily at the dirt around the rubber. Mr. Henry went out and talked to him. "Don't get down on yourself, boy. That was just a fat 3 and 0 pitch. He couldn't have hit your smoker. You'll get him next time around."

The words seemed to calm Cal, and he pitched well after that. He only allowed one more hit and, believe it or not, I got it. And believe it or not, it was a leg hit. I hit a ground ball to short. I don't know if Kevin backed up on it or what he did. I didn't look to see. I just ran to first like there were hot coals under my feet.

"You ran that out like Cool Papa himself, boy," Mr. Henry shouted at me.

I never got off first, though. Cal got Kim to pop up and Aaron lined out to Art and that was the old ball game. We won it 2–0 because Aaron kept striking out people. No one even got a foul tick.

In the middle of the third inning Chuck Axelrod told his crew to stop shooting. They had enough game footage. But he said not to pack up just yet. There was something else he wanted to shoot.

When the three-inning game was over, Chuck Axelrod slapped Aaron on the back. "You've got one heckuvan arm on you, son. You'll be pitching for the Tigers one of these days. You're the grandson of Buck McHenry all right. Now don't anyone leave. We've got one more thing to shoot."

I was hoping he'd interview me again, because I wanted to point out, humbly, if I could, that we could have beat Baer Machine with only two players, a pitcher and a catcher.

But Chuck Axelrod didn't want any more interviews. He wanted shots of kids shaking hands. Like the end of a hockey game.

The Baer Machine guys were okay. "I bet you're glad to be shaking with your meat hand, Jayce," Tug said to me.

I'd forgot all about my left hand hurting. It was red and puffy, but the more they struck out, the less it hurt.

"Isn't he great, Tugger?"

"Best I ever seen," Tug said.

Good old Tug. He was classy. I heard him say to Aaron, "You're good, man."

"Thanks," Aaron said, shyly.

The guys shook hands with Kim without making too many cracks. After all, she had got a solid hit off Cal. When Cal got to her, he said, "That was a lucky hit you got off me."

"No, it wasn't," Kim said.

The guys laughed. They were impressed with her. Heck, I was too.

After taping the handshaking, the crew packed up their equipment and Chuck Axelrod went over to each kid and thanked him for helping out. To Kim, he said, "Honey, I've got to get to the station and start editing. Do you know how to get home from here?"

"I'm okay," she said, blushing. I don't think she liked being called honey in front of everyone. Certainly not after scoring the winning run. Or maybe it was his suggesting she didn't know how to get home.

"I'll call you from Detroit. There's tuna fish in the fridge." He sort of looked embarrassed. "I've got a housekeeper hired but she can't start till next week," he said to us, but mostly to Mr. Henry. "Listen, all of you, thanks again. And Mr. McHenry, a special thanks to you. You're going to do a lot for kids' baseball in Arborville. In fact," he said with a grin, "between the two of us we just might put the kids' baseball program here on the national map. The Buck McHenry story is the kind of story that could get picked up by the network and the wire services. All right, everyone, remember, *Sportsline*, Channel 4. Nine o'clock tonight!"

As though we would forget.

Chuck Axelrod ran, he didn't walk, he ran over to his Lincoln. He shouted something at the Channel 4 van. Then he burned rubber out of the parking lot. The Channel 4 van followed him out almost as fast.

"Your dad always move that fast?" Tug asked Kim.

"When he's late for a show he does."

"How long is it going to take him to edit the tapes?" I asked.

"A couple of hours."

"He's late all right," Pete said.

"I gotta go home and tell my folks about this. My grandpa too," Kevin said. "He always watches *Sportsline*." Kevin ran for his bike. The others walked to their bikes.

Mr. Henry said to Aaron, "We got to get going too, boy. We got to get your bike at Jason's house."

It was like he'd lost himself in the game, but now that the game was over he was worried again about the TV show. I didn't know what he was worried about. Those scrapes with the law were nothing. Absolutely nothing. Grabbing four dollars when crooks owed you a hundred? *They* were the ones who broke the law.

He couldn't get Aaron moving though. Aaron didn't want it to end. None of us did. Kim pounded her glove. I thought about her going back alone to that huge empty house.

"You want to eat at our house?" I asked her. She shook her head.

"It'll be okay. My mom's a great cook."

"We've got food."

"Tuna fish," I said.

"I like tuna fish."

"Kim could eat at our house, couldn't she, Grampa? And Jason too. Then we could all watch the show together. My grandma's a great cook."

"I couldn't, Aaron. I got to be home to get the phone calls from kids," I said.

"Let's go get your bike, boy," Mr. Henry said. "We can ride over to Jason's house in my truck."

"What about the equipment bag?" Kim asked.

In the excitement, we'd forgotten to put the bats, balls, and catcher's gear back in the bag.

"The three of you pack it up," Mr. Henry said.

While we were packing up the equipment bag, the Baer Machine kids who were still there came over to us.

"Mr. uh . . . Henry," Cal said. "Can we ask you something?"

"Of course you can, Calvin."

"If The Grandstand doesn't come up with a full team, I know my dad would like to have Aaron play for us."

Kim and I looked at each other. This we hadn't expected. We looked at Aaron. He was stuffing a bat in the bag. "I'm goin' to play for my grampa," he said softly without looking up.

"Sure, man. But I know my dad would really like having Mr. Henry help him coach."

Silence. Then Aaron picked up the shin guards and put them in the bag. "Jason, Kim, and I are friends," Aaron said. "Teammates," he added.

"But suppose you don't get a team?"

"We'll get a team," Kim said, glaring at Cal. She looked like she was ready to punch him.

Cal backed off. Mr. Henry smiled. "Boys, I think we'd best leave things as they be. You've got a team. You've got the chemistry." He cleared his throat. "Only thing is when you come up against a pitcher who throws real hard, all you want to do is get wood on the ball. Let his speed do your work, let his speed be your power. You kids got that bag packed?"

"Yes, sir," we said.

"Put it in the truck."

He might have just given them good coaching,

but when he told us to put the bag in his truck, he was really signing on as our coach. Coaches kept equipment bags. It was like signing a contract. Now all that had to happen to make this day a complete success was for the phone to start ringing after the *Sportsline* show.

18

"See ya, Aaron."

"See ya, Jason. See ya, Kim."

"See ya, Aaron."

"See ya, Mr. Henry."

The yellow pickup with the bike and the equipment bag in back left our driveway. Kim and I watched it make a right turn on Ferdon and disappear. Then Kim got on her bike.

"Do you know how to get home from here?" I asked her.

"Sure."

"How?"

She looked around and then pointed in the wrong direction.

I laughed. "I'll bike you home. Just let me tell my folks where I'm going. They'll be sore if I disappear on them again. Come in for a second."

"Jason, my dad'll be calling to see if I got home okay."

"It's just for a second. They won't believe me when I tell them what happened. You've got to confirm it."

"All right, but I can't stay."

Sounds of typing came from Dad's den. The radio was playing in the kitchen. Mom had her back to us and was fiddling with it when we came in. The dining-room table was set for three.

"Boo," I said.

Mom jumped. She's easy to scare.

"Thanks a lot, Jason." She flipped off the radio.

"You won't believe what happened, Mom. The three of us beat nine Baer Machine kids in a three-inning game. Aaron threw nothing but strike-outs."

"Is that a good thing to throw?"

Kim gasped.

"You see what I have to live with," I said. "Can I get Dad? We want to tell you what happened. The ball game was only part of it."

"He's working on something important, Jason. Tell me."

"Okay. Not only did we win our game but we're all going to be on TV. And Mr. Henry was wonderful, wasn't he, Kim?"

She nodded. "I gotta go, Jason."

"Wait a second. Mr. Henry told Kim's dad what it was like to play in the old Negro leagues. Mom, it was awful. They cheated those guys all the time. You'll see it on *Sportsline* tonight."

"Jason, my father's going to call soon."

"Mom, do we have enough food to invite Kim for supper?"

I blurted it out. It was wrong of me, I know. You're not supposed to invite kids for dinner without asking first if it's okay. What could my mom say in front of Kim? No? It was embarrassing to Mom and embarrassing to Kim. I think the only reason I blurted it out was because I was still bothered at the idea of her eating alone in that big house. Especially after a victory like that.

If Mom was embarrassed or annoyed, she didn't show it. She's real good that way. "It's just lasagna, Kim, and we do have more than enough, as a matter of fact."

"She makes great lasagna, Kim. Change your mind?"

Kim wouldn't look at either of us. "I've got to go," she mumbled and headed for the door.

"Why do you have to go? No one's home in your house."

"Is that right?" Mom said. "No one's home?"

Kim kept going.

"That's right," I said. "No one's home except some tuna fish."

Kim was at the door.

"Her dad's editing the tape in Detroit. Her mom lives in Birmingham."

"Wait a second, Kim," Mom called out.

Kim stopped.

"We really do have more than enough lasagna, Kim. Please stay, unless, of course, you don't like lasagna," Mom said gently.

"I like lasagna," Kim said. Her face got all red. "We have it a lot."

"Frozen, I bet," I said.

"Jason, for goodness' sakes. What kind of manners are those? I'm sure Kim's father is busy and doesn't have time to cook. We'd love to have you, Kim."

Kim bit her lip. I think she wanted to stay but wasn't sure my mom really wanted her to. Maybe if we got away from talking about just feeding her.

"You could look over my baseball cards afterward," I said. "You could tell me what you think my collection's worth."

Like she'd be doing me a favor if she stayed.

"Kim's got over thirty thousand cards, Mom. She's got a 1952 Mickey Mantle. Signed."

"Who's Mickey Mantle?" Mom said.

"C'mon, Mom. You know who Mickey Mantle is."

"Is he a pitcher or a batter?"

Kim laughed. Mom couldn't have said anything better to relax Kim. The sad part was that Mom didn't do it on purpose. She really wanted to know.

"C'mon, stay for supper," I said. "Then I'll bike you home."

Kim looked up questioningly at Mom.

"We'd really love to have you eat with us, Kim," Mom said.

Kim nodded quickly. "Thanks, Mrs. Ross. But I better call my dad and see if it's okay with him."

"How are you going to call him?" I said. "He won't be in Detroit yet."

"I'll call him in his car."

"Neat. Ask him where he is."

It was a regular number she punched up. Kim asked him right off where he was. I heard his laugh. "No," she said, "that's not why. Jason wants to know." Pause. "I'll tell him. Dad, Mrs. Ross has invited me to stay for supper. Can I? Pause. "Thanks. Okay. 'Bye."

"He's just passing Metro airport. And I can stay."

"Great. Now both of you wash up," Mom said.

We washed up. Mom pried Dad out of his den and we sat down to eat some great lasagna. I spent more time talking than eating. I told them everything. Mr. Henry, the TV crew and taping, the game, Baer Machine wanting Aaron to pitch for them, Aaron saying he wanted to play with his friends. And Kim confirmed every detail so they knew I wasn't making it up.

Only once did Dad interrupt, and that was when I mentioned that our phone number was going to be broadcast on the air.

"You're joking," Dad said.

"No."

Dad groaned. Mom quickly changed the subject and asked Kim if she wanted a career in television like her father. Kim shook her head.

"What would you like to be when you grow up?" Mom asked her.

"A teacher."

"I know what I'm going to be," I said.

"What?" Kim asked.

"I'm going to run a baseball card store like The Grandstand. I think it's great to do what you like and be paid for it too. Maybe when Jim retires I'll take over—oh no!"

"What's the matter?" Dad said.

"Jim doesn't know The Grandstand's going

to be mentioned on *Sportsline* tonight. He doesn't know anything about what happened today." I jumped up from the table.

"Where're you going?" Dad asked.

"I'm going to call him."

"You sit right down and finish eating first," Mom said.

"But—"

"Sit down and finish dinner, Jason," Dad said.

I sat down and finished dinner. But what a thing to forget. Luckily The Grandstand stays open late on Saturdays. When I was done, and Mom didn't make me wait for dessert, I called The Grandstand and got Jim. I told him all that happened. While I talked I could hear him doing business. When I got to the Buck McHenry part (which was news to him) and then to the video-taping at the park and Chuck Axelrod mention-ing The Grandstand on camera, Jim stopped doing business.

"Jason," he said, "you're making this up."

"I'm not. You know who Kim Axelrod is. His daughter. She's here. Ask her. Kim, c'mere. He doesn't believe me. You tell him."

"Jason, no . . ." She shook her head.

"C'mon, he's our sponsor. Tell him." I stuck the phone in her hands. What a time to be shy.

"Hi," she said timidly. And then I didn't hear

200

what Jim said but she told him exactly what I had said. When I got back on, Jim was so excited, he was spluttering.

"Jason . . . I apologize. . . . You were right from the beginning. About Buck McHenry . . . about everything. The Grandstand's going to be on TV. Oh, too much, too much. I'm going to close early and go home and watch it. Jason, oh Jason, I'll . . . I'll talk to you later."

"He's closing the store to go home and watch the show," I announced.

"Where are you going to watch it, Kim?" Mom asked.

"Home."

"Alone?" Mom said. She smiled. "That doesn't sound so good. I think the team ought to watch it together. Why don't you stay here and watch it and afterward Jason's father will drive you and your bike home."

What Mom said gave me goose pimples. She was right. The team ought to watch it together. And handle the phone calls together. But there was another person on that team.

"Mom, Dad, can Kim and I bike over to Aaron's house and bring him here? He should be here too. And we could drive them both home afterward, couldn't we?"

"It's all right with me," Dad said, "but why

do you have to bike there? Why can't you phone him and ask him to come here?"

"He won't know how to get here. And I can't ask Mr. Henry. He's spent so much time on us already. It wouldn't be fair. Kim and I could go get him."

"Where do they live?" Mom asked.

"On North Fourth Avenue. We can go right down Washtenaw. You want to come, don't you?" I asked Kim.

"Yes." She looked embarrassed. "But I better call my father and tell him I'm going to watch the show here. He'll be calling home the second it's over."

"Boy, you are really on a short leash."

She blushed. "No, it's just that . . ." She shrugged. "He and I are alone."

Silence. Then Dad said, "Go call him, Kim."

"It's long distance. It's Detroit, Mr. Ross."

Dad smiled. "That's all right. We're the same area code."

"You sure know a lot of phone numbers," I said as she punched up Channel 4, Detroit. The only number I knew by heart was The Grandstand. And sometimes ours.

"Hi. This is Kim Axelrod. Is my dad—?" (Pause.) "Oh. Could you tell him I'm going to watch the show at Jason's house?" (Pause.) "He knows who Jason is." (Pause.) "It's the same phone number that's going to be on the show. Right. Thanks."

"Your dad busy?"

"He hasn't finished editing."

"What a job. Let's go."

"Jason," Dad said, "it'll be getting dark soon. Please ride on the sidewalks."

"We will, Dad. We'll be careful."

19

The way to Aaron's house from my house was pretty much the same as from her house to his. Except she lived on the other side of Washtenaw. Kim and I biked down Washtenaw, past the First Presbyterian Church, then across campus and downtown past City Hall, the fire station, and then into the old part of town.

We got slowed up between campus and downtown, where a lot of people were out walking. It was nice weather and dusk is a pretty time to walk in Arborville. And then we hit red lights on Liberty, Washington, and Huron. By the time we got to Aaron's neighborhood, it had gotten dark. But there was a nice full moon out. And Aaron's street was bathed in moonlight.

I pointed out the old stone Underground Railroad house to Kim.

"I bet you didn't have anything like that in Birmingham."

"I don't think so."

"There's Aaron's house."

"Where?"

"The little white one with the fence in front."

"What's that noise?"

"What noise?"

"Don't you hear it?"

"No. Yes. I do now."

It was a muffled *thump, thump, thump.* Then a long pause. And then *thump, thump, thump.* It seemed to be coming from behind Aaron's house. There was something familiar about it. Like I'd heard it before. And then it hit me. I knew exactly what it was. I grinned.

"You know what it is?" she asked.

"Yep. It's Aaron. We'll sneak up on him and surprise him. Let's be quiet."

"What's he doing?"

"You'll see in a second," I whispered. "Be quiet."

I unlatched the front gate with the WELCOME. THE MACK HENRYS. hanging from it. We walked our bikes in and then I held my finger to my lips. I laid my bike down gently, noiselessly. Kim did the same.

Lights were on in the house. As we crept along the side of the house and got closer to the backyard, the thumps sounded larger. They were in series of threes. Three thumps. Nothing for a few seconds. Then three more thumps.

Kim looked really baffled. I restrained a laugh.

We tiptoed underneath their windows. There were rectangles of light on the ground. We sneaked around and between them, like doing a ski slalom.

In a few seconds we were standing next to one of the steel supports that held up the back porch. I heard a sharp intake of breath from Kim. There was Aaron in the moonlight firing baseballs at the mattress hanging from the shed.

He'd fire three pitches and then run and get the balls and come back and fire three more pitches. It was beautiful. The kind of thing sports legends are made of. How did Aaron Henry, winner of twenty games in his first season in the majors, become such a great pitcher?

Well, when Aaron Henry was a kid growing up in Arborville, Michigan, on moonlit evenings he used to pitch baseballs at a mattress his grandfather, the great Buck McHenry, had hung on a shed in their backyard. Over and over, hundreds of pitches, he would throw to a bull's-eye on the mattress.

"I owe everything I am today to my grampa," Aaron would tell the reporters.

I was making up a story, I knew, but it could

happen. I looked at Kim. Her eyes were shining. "He's great, Jason," she whispered.

"How about when I say three, we both yell: 'Strike three. You're out'?"

She laughed. "Okay." She was game for anything.

"One, two—" I stopped. Above us a door had opened, floorboards creaked. We looked at each other. We couldn't shout at Aaron now.

"We're right under their back porch," I whispered.

And then Mrs. Henry's voice sounded, inches above us, it felt like.

"You have to call him in and tell him, Mr. Henry," she said quietly.

Thump, thump, thump went the three balls.

"What's he going to think of me, Jessie?"

"Jessie's Mrs. Henry, his wife," I whispered to Kim.

"He'll think the same of you as what he thought before. But you've got to tell him. After that, we can figure out a plan of action about those others."

What was she talking about?

"There's nothing to figure," Mr. Henry said softly. "Your man made the biggest fool of himself that he could make with those kids and that TV camera."

Kim and I stared at each other. What was he talking about? He had been a wonderful coach in our little practice game. And he had given a great interview to her dad. He would be letting people all over Michigan know about the old Negro leagues.

"Telling those kids I played with Satchel Paige and Josh Gibson and Cool Papa Bell. I even told them what life was like in the leagues."

What was wrong with him telling us that?

"Did you tell them the truth, Mr. Henry?"

"The truth of what I've heard. Not what I've ever been."

I froze. *Thump, thump, thump* went my heart in rhythm with Aaron's pitches.

"And the thing of it was," Mr. Henry said, "I made it real. Real to them and real to me. So real there were moments I thought maybe I *was* Buck McHenry."

I grabbed onto one of the steel supports. I couldn't believe what I'd just heard. And then I thought, maybe I didn't hear it right. I looked at Kim. Her face was scared. It was the first time I'd seen her look scared. I'd heard it right.

"And that wasn't even the worst of it, Jessie. The worst of it came when I started tellin' the TV camera and the whole world how Buck McHenry got in trouble with the law. He asked me that, Mr. Chuck Axelrod did, and I answered. I went that far, Jessie."

"Well, did you know why he got in trouble with the law?"

"Of course I didn't know, woman," he said angrily. "I told them what happened to me once when I was pitching for that semipro team. How I wouldn't throw a game on purpose and how the sheriff chased us out of town. But Jessie, that happened to me. It didn't happen to the great Buck McHenry."

"It might've, Mr. Henry."

"Woman, the great Buck McHenry wasn't throwing games in cow towns. He was pitching in Yankee Stadium and the Polo Grounds. In the Negro leagues. Pitchin' for the Grays and the Crawfords. Pitching in front of big crowds. Jessie, I *saw* Buck McHenry pitch in Detroit. I *saw* Satchel Paige pitch. I *saw* Gibson and Judy Johnson and Cool Papa. I paid money and I sat in the bleachers and I *saw*. I saw and never was."

He started to cry. Right there inches over our heads, Mr. Henry started to sob. The sound of his sobs tore through the floor and into my heart. Kim put her hand on mine, tugging at me. I brushed her hand off. I thought she was trying to comfort me.

"Jason," she whispered, "we've got to get out of here."

Of course we had to get out of here, but how? They'd hear us if we took one single step. We were right underneath them. And if they discovered us hiding here, then what? That would be worse than anything. They'd know we'd overheard.

"Mr. Henry, you best hush now. The boy is coming."

Aaron had stopped throwing. He had the three balls and was running toward the house. Kim and I froze. Aaron would be coming within a few feet of us. He did. He ran past us and took the steps two at a time and disappeared. Then we heard the screen door at the top of the stairs open and shut.

"Grampa, what time's it?" Aaron asked.

Mr. Henry cleared his throat. "It's not show time yet, boy, if that's what you're after."

"You all right, Grampa?"

"Sure I am."

"You sound funny."

"I got something stuck in my throat."

"Aaron, where are you going now?" Mrs. Henry said.

"See if it's on, Grandma."

"You just heard your grampa say that—"

The inside house door shut. A second later the TV was turned on in the other room.

"He doesn't want to miss a second of it, does he?" Mr. Henry said. We heard him blow his nose.

"You've got to talk to him before it starts, Mr. Henry."

"I can't, Jessie."

"Jason." Kim tugged at my sleeve again.

I shook my head. We'd had our chance when Aaron was clomping up the steps. That noise would have covered us. Now we'd have to wait for more noise.

"It's going to be all right, Mr. Henry. You told the truth to that TV camera. Maybe it wasn't Buck McHenry's truth, but it was your truth."

"Jessie, truth is a lie when it comes from a liar's mouth."

"Mr. Henry, truth is truth no matter who says it. All you did was make up a story so you *could* tell the truth. Furthermore, Mr. Henry, you weren't alone in making up that story. You had help. Who was it first called you Buck McHenry?"

"Jason."

I winced.

"Yes, but who was it made it official? Me! It was me who told them you were Buck McHenry. And why did I do it? Because it was helping the boy. The boy's alive now. He's got friends. He's on a baseball team. And you're going to coach him. That's what's important, Mr. Henry. That's what you've got to keep your eye on."

"You don't understand, Jessie. There isn't any team. There's just three youngsters who think I'm Buck McHenry. And if there is a team, the boy isn't goin' to want me to coach him. When he finds out, he's going to be ashamed of me and he'll be right. I'm ashamed of myself. And this Axelrod fellow? What's goin' to happen to him when he goes on TV with this pack of lies? When the truth comes out, he'll probably get fired."

I hadn't even thought of that. I turned to look at Kim. My right elbow banged into one of the steel poles.

"Did you hear something outside, Mr. Henry?" Mrs. Henry asked.

My heart thumped so hard I thought they could also hear that. Kim was rigid.

Mr. Henry said, "People will be calling the TV station. People who knew Buck McHenry. Who might still know him. For all I know Buck McHenry himself'll call in. If he's still alive. That darn baseball card of Jason's. That's where it all started. If it wasn't for that card, none of this would've happened."

"Well, it's happened, Mr. Henry. And the worst possible thing would be for Aaron to hear about it from someone else. All you got to do now is . . ."

We lost her next words, because just then there was a blast of TV noise. The door had opened. Over the noise we heard Aaron say, "Grandma, can I get somethin' to eat?"

We took off then. Kim and me, running close to the house. We didn't avoid the rectangles of light. If they didn't hear us, they wouldn't look for us.

We ran to the front of the house, grabbed our bikes, and ran them to the front gate. Kim unlatched the gate and went through it. I latched it behind us. That was risky, but I hate leaving people's gates open. She waited for me. She didn't know how to get home.

"This way," I said, and those would be the only words either of us said until we reached Washtenaw and Devonshire.

We didn't talk because there was nothing to say. One moment you're sitting on top of the world, the next moment you're living in a nightmare.

20

We biked hard. Mostly because Kim was pushing it. I didn't know what the big rush was. What was going to happen was going to happen. Fate was in charge of us.

We biked past teenagers, college students, people getting in and out of cars, taxicabs. We biked past people waiting at bus stops, waiting to get into a theater. We biked past people eating ice-cream cones outside a fancy ice-cream store. We biked past people sitting on stone benches. It seemed like half of Arborville was hanging out that night. Which was okay since it meant they wouldn't be watching *Sportsline*.

When we came to the spot where Devonshire came into Washtenaw, I pointed it out to Kim just the way earlier today I'd pointed it out to Aaron. Although now that seemed like years ago.

"You live four houses up."

She nodded, and when there was a break in the traffic she bounced her bike over the curb and crossed Washtenaw, standing up, pedaling hard. I watched her for a moment and then I pedaled slowly home. I was running out of gas. I was exhausted.

When I got to our house, I put my bike in the garage. Then I went and sat on the steps to get some breath and calm inside my body. I must have sat on our front steps for five minutes before I felt calmer. Then I went inside the house.

The TV set was on. Mom and Dad were watching it.

"Has it started?" I asked, alarmed.

"Not yet. There's still a few minutes," Dad said. "Where are Kim and Aaron?"

"They're not coming."

"I thought you were going to watch the show together."

"We're not."

I sat down on the sofa. Not facing the TV. I didn't want to watch the TV.

"Are you all right, Jason?" Mom asked.

"Sure."

"What's the matter, Jason?" Dad asked. "What happened?"

You can never fool people who love you.

"Everything's the matter," I said. "Everything." And then I started to cry. Out of nowhere I started to cry.

Mom came and put her arms around me. "Jason, whatever it is, it's all right."

"It's not all right," I sobbed. "And it never will be."

I wept. Like a baby in his mother's arms. Finally, I forced myself to stop.

"Do you want to tell us what's going on?" Dad asked.

"No." I wiped my face on my Baer Machine shirt.

They didn't say anything. Just looked at me with concern.

"All right. I'll tell you."

And then, not looking at them, looking at the carpet at my feet, I told them that Mr. Henry wasn't really Buck McHenry. That he'd gone along with it because I wanted him to and because of Aaron. I told my folks about Aaron. And I told them how Kim and I heard Mr. Henry confess the truth on his back porch. And how he cried because he'd told these lies to the camera and how scared he was now that they would come out. He was scared too for Aaron to find out. What would Aaron think of him? What would everyone in Arborville think of him? What

216

would the Baer Machine kids who all went to Eberwoods School where he worked think of him? Because sooner or later the truth would come out. Wouldn't it, Dad? Wouldn't it, Mom? Wouldn't the truth come out? On TV, in the newspapers, everywhere?

They didn't say anything. Which meant it would.

I almost started to cry again. Mom got me a Kleenex.

"Blow your nose," she said.

"None of it would have happened if only I'd minded my own business. Thanks." I blew my nose.

"You made a mistake, Jason, that's all," Mom said. "It was a mistake of enthusiasm. You just wanted things to be a certain way."

"You wrote a scenario for real life," Dad said, "and real life came and bopped you on the nose."

"I wouldn't mind it if it was just my nose that got bopped."

Dad laughed. "You'll be all right, Jason. And your Mr. Henry will be all right too." He looked at his watch. "Come. There may still be time to do something about it."

"What can we do?"

Dad lead the way to the kitchen. "Call Chuck Axelrod and ask him to kill the story."

"It's too late."

"Maybe not. Maybe the story's late in the show. There are commercials to get through at the beginning of every show."

"Who're you calling?"

"Directory assistance for Channel 4."

"What are you going to say to him?"

"I'm not going to say anything. You are. You'll talk to him."

"What will I say?"

"Just what you told us. I'd like the phone number for Channel 4, Detroit, operator."

"Suppose he doesn't believe me?"

"Then you'll have done all you can do." Dad repeated the phone number out loud to himself and started dialing again.

"It's ringing." He handed me the phone. "I'll go upstairs and get on the phone in the hall."

The phone rang at Channel 4. Dad started down the back hall to the stairs.

"WDIV, Channel 4 Detroit . . ." a telephone voice began.

"It's starting," Mom called out.

"Can I help you?"

"No," I said.

I hung up the phone and went into the living room.

Chuck Axelrod was on the screen, smiling into the camera saying, "On this week's edition of *Sportsline* we have a unique, heartwarming baseball story for you. It's local too. So stay tuned for *Sportsline!*"

"Dad," I called, "it's too late."

"I see that," Dad said. He was in the room. He came and stood next to me. On the screen there appeared a rapid succession of sports shots. Great plays in basketball, football, baseball, hockey.

And then an announcer's voice said over them, "*Sportsline* with Chuck Axelrod is brought to you by . . ." There followed the list of sponsors. Beer, cars, airlines, automobile tires, riding lawn mowers . . .

"Both of you, sit down," Mom said.

Dad sat down. I didn't. I wanted to run upstairs and jump into bed and pull the covers over my head.

"Come on, Jason," Dad said. "Sit down."

I shook my head.

"Life is going to go on, Jason. It's going to be all right."

No, I thought, it wouldn't be all right. Not for Mr. Henry. Not for Aaron. Not for Chuck Axelrod. And not for me. The only thing that could save the four of us now was if a bolt of lightning hit the TV station, or an earthquake swallowed up Detroit.

On the TV the commercials went on and on and on. For once I wished they'd never end.

21

But end they did and once more Chuck Axelrod's face appeared on the screen.

"Before we get to tonight's feature story," he said, "we have highlights of this afternoon's Tiger victory over the California Angels."

That's what they always do to you on TV. Tell you something is coming up and you keep tuned and then something else comes. In this case, a highlights tape.

Usually I love highlights—the great catches, home runs, steals—but right now I wasn't seeing them. I was picturing in my mind Aaron in his living room with Mr. and Mrs. Henry watching their TV set. Had Mr. Henry told Aaron the truth yet? Probably. Was Aaron sore at his grampa? Was he ashamed of him the way Mr. Henry said he'd be? That would be awful. Was Aaron sore at me? My head felt like it would burst.

"Jason, go to the refrigerator and get yourself some juice," Mom said.

"I'm not thirsty."

Next I pictured Kim in her big empty living room watching and waiting for the axe to fall. On her father. Because when the show was over, people were going to start calling Channel 4 to say that Mr. Henry wasn't Buck McHenry at all and that Chuck Axelrod was full of hot air and wrong facts.

Maybe Buck McHenry's family would call. Maybe, like Mr. Henry said, Buck McHenry himself would call. Oh God, why couldn't I turn my mind off?

Finally the highlights were over.

"I guess I will get a glass of juice," I said.

But then there were more commercials so I didn't have to leave. Mom turned to Dad. "Dick, isn't there something else on TV we could watch?"

"Jean, we have to watch this. If for no other reason than to know what Mr. Henry is in for."

"And Chuck Axelrod," I said.

"Yes, and Chuck Axelrod too."

"And Aaron. Especially if they haven't told him."

"Jason, stop picking on yourself."

"Dad, I started it all."

"You may have started it, but Mr. Henry picked up the ball and ran with it. He didn't have to go along with it, you know."

"He did though." My voice was getting hysterical. "For Aaron's sake."

"Jason, it's no one's fault. It's just something that happened," Mom said.

"It wouldn't have happened if I'd kept my big mouth shut and not tried to write scenarios, as Dad said."

"Shsh," Dad said.

The commercials ended. For a second the screen was blank and then—I gasped. There, larger than life, was my Buck McHenry card.

"Today's feature story," Chuck Axelrod's voice said as we looked at the card, "begins with a very unusual baseball card. A card of a famous pitcher in the old Negro leagues, the only organized baseball leagues black men could play in till Jackie Robinson broke the color barrier.

"This man's name was Buck McHenry, and he was ranked along with the great Satchel Paige as one of the great right-handed pitchers in the old Negro leagues."

There now flashed on the screen a series of old black-and-white pictures of stars from the old Negro leagues. Between the time he left Sampson Park and the show went on the air,

Chuck Axelrod had done research, got pictures, facts. No wonder he was famous. He worked hard. I felt so sorry for what was going to happen to him.

"McHenry pitched against immortals like Cool Papa Bell, Josh Gibson, Martin Dihigo, Oscar Huddleston, Buck Leonard . . . the list could go on and on. Unlike many of these great black ballplayers, Buck McHenry had only a three-year career in the Negro leagues. But a tremendous three years they were. In each of those years, Buck McHenry won thirty games or more. And there were those who claimed his fastball was better than Satchel Paige's. Faster than Bob Feller's, who was the king of smoke in the major leagues."

The Buck McHenry card came back on the screen, only this time it was the stats side. You could just about read it.

"From the back of Buck McHenry's baseball card we learn that after he suddenly and inexplicably quit baseball, he took a job as a school custodian right here in our own state of Michigan."

Chuck Axelrod was back on camera. He had jumped right over the scrapes with the law. For a split second hope rose inside me. But then I remembered that Mr. Henry had covered that in the interview taped in the park.

"Dad, could Mr. Henry go to jail for pretending to be Buck McHenry?"

"No. Shsh."

"If he did, would you defend him?"

"Yes. Be quiet."

Well, that was something anyway.

On the screen Chuck Axelrod was saying, "Today, on a Little League baseball diamond . . ."

"I've got to go to the bathroom," I announced. I really did. I wasn't fooling. That sometimes happens when I'm scared.

The sound of the TV followed me all the way to the toilet off the kitchen.

". . . in Arborville we *thought* we had rediscovered Buck McHenry."

I got as far as the bathroom door when I heard "we *thought* we had rediscovered." He had stressed "thought," not we.

I ran back into the living room. "Did you hear what he said? He said that—"

I stopped and stared. There we all were. On TV. The Baer Machine guys—Kevin and Cal and Tim and Tug and Art and Greg and Pete—and there I was and there were Aaron and Kim and then the camera zoomed in on Mr. Henry, who was talking to us.

"Jason, you're catching," he was saying. "Get

your gear on, boy. Aaron, you're pitching. Young lady, you're going to have to play everywhere else. You just play each . . ."

Chuck Axelrod's voice came back over Mr. Henry's.

"*Sportsline* had received a tip that Buck McHenry had changed his name to Mack Henry and was the custodian at Eberwoods School in Arborville. And further, that he was going to coach a new team in the Arborville eleven-year-old league called The Grandstand.

"This tip came from an Arborville youngster who collected baseball cards, who discovered the Buck McHenry card and decided Mr. Mack Henry was Buck McHenry . . ."

My heart pounded.

"There you are, Jason," Mom said. She wasn't even listening. She was just waiting to see me on TV.

And there I was, warming up Aaron.

"This *Sportsline* feature story belongs to that youngster who collected the Buck McHenry card as well as to two others. Two young people new to Arborville, one a girl named Kim Axelrod, my daughter . . ."

There was a shot of Kim smacking her fist in her glove.

" . . . and a boy named Aaron Henry who formerly played Little League baseball in Tennessee. Aaron Henry was recovering from a family tragedy."

How did he find out about that? How did he learn that maybe Mr. Henry wasn't— And then it hit me. Why Kim had wanted to get away from Mr. Henry's house so fast. And why she had pedaled so hard to her house. She was a hundred steps ahead of me.

"Aaron had lost his father and mother and older brother in an automobile accident and had moved up to Michigan to live with his grandparents and start a new life up here. Our third youngster is our card collector, Jason Ross."

I thought I would faint. Blood rushed to my temples. There was a close-up of me catching. I was glad I had my mask on.

"Earlier that day Jason Ross had been cut from another team . . ."

Why did he have to mention that?

". . . in fact, the very team the newly formed Grandstand team was having a practice game against this afternoon. Unfortunately The Grandstand only had three players. But they did have the great Buck McHenry coaching them—or so we thought at the time."

A hundred steps ahead of me? A thousand. Light-years.

"However, life doesn't always have a storybook happy ending—or does it?" Chuck Axelrod went on. "Just before we went on the air I learned from a close source"—very close, I thought—"that Mr. Mack Henry wasn't the great Buck McHenry after all. Yes, he was a school custodian in Arborville. Yes, he had played baseball in the South before integration. But never in the Negro leagues. Mack Henry was one of those hundreds of young black ballplayers who traveled from town to town in old cars, old busses, trying to pick up a dollar or two playing local teams, and playing under all kinds of circumstances, on all kinds of fields, in front of all kinds of spectators. Often taking all kinds of abuse. You see, folks, the history of the black baseball player in America is more than a history of the Negro leagues and its great stars—the Satchel Paiges, the Josh Gibsons, the Cool Papa Bells, the Buck McHenrys. It's also the story and history of those who received no glory, who received no pay, who played in bumpy cow pastures in town after town, challenging the local teams, playing because they loved to play baseball. Today perhaps these men would be called journeyman players in the major leagues, .250 hitters in the major leagues. But they'd be up there, make no mistake about that. Not stars.

Not Hank Aarons, Ricky Hendersons, Willie Mays, but firmly placed in the constellation of all those who contributed to America's national pastime. They never had a chance to get their names and statistics onto the bubble gum baseball cards that America's youth collect today with such knowledgeability. But these men belong there. They played, lived, and died believing that America's national game was theirs too. And, as it turned out, it was."

"He would have made a fantastic trial lawyer," Dad said softly.

"No, Mack Henry, custodian at Eberwoods School, wasn't the legendary Buck McHenry that young Jason Ross thought he was. He was, if anything, something more. For today on a Little League diamond in Arborville, Michigan"— Chuck Axelrod broke into a wide grin—"Mr. Mack Henry, an old semipro ballplayer from the South, did something we suspect the great Buck McHenry never did."

"What was that?" Mom asked.

"Shsh," Dad said. The picture on the screen changed.

22

The game had started. Aaron was pitching. Kevin was taking strike after strike. And Chuck Axelrod was saying, "What Mr. Mack Henry did today was take three kids and coach them to victory over nine. Three players beat nine."

There was a shot of Kim getting on base. And then of Aaron hitting his home run. And Aaron striking out player after player and then shots of all of us shaking hands, and Tug saying simply, "You're good, man."

And then as the handshaking went on, a shot of Mr. Henry smiling as he watched everyone shake hands. "We don't know where the real Buck McHenry is today," Chuck Axelrod said quietly. "We hope he's alive, well, and happy. We do know where the real Mack Henry is.

"He's coaching a team called The Grandstand in the Arborville eleven-year-old league. And it's a team looking for more players."

Now Chuck Axelrod was back on camera and in the studio.

"So we end a rather unusual *Sportsline* feature story with an appeal: If there are any eleven-year-old youngsters in Arborville watching this show right now who are not presently on a team and want to play for The Grandstand and be coached by Mr. Mack Henry, you are hereby asked to call Jason Ross at . . ."

And then he gave our number. Right there on TV. It was even shown!

Dad groaned. Mom laughed. My heart thumped with each digit. Then he repeated our phone number again and my heart thumped some more.

After that, commercials came on and Dad turned off the set. Then he looked at me. His face was somber. "Well, Jason, you did it. Thanks to you, our home phone number was broadcast to the whole world."

"Just southeast Michigan, Dick," Mom said.

And with that Dad started to laugh. And I laughed with him. "Wasn't it great what he did, Dad? He never mentioned what happened at all. Mr. Henry making that speech. He never showed it. You know, it's too bad in a way, because it was a great speech Mr. Henry made to us about a game he played in a long time ago."

"Jason, if I know Chuck Axelrod, and I think I do after tonight's show, the way he could make a story out of a nonstory, he'll use Mr. Henry's speech some other place, some other time."

"He made something out of nothing, didn't he? Just the way the old black ballplayers did. Chuck Axelrod's a genius. Don't you think he's a genius, Mom?"

"Yes. Certainly. But how did he find out—"

"It had to be Kim. I'm going to call her right now. She's a genius too."

I ran to the phone. Just as I got there it rang. I picked it up. "Kim," I said, "you did it!"

"Is this Jason Ross?" A strange voice asked.

"Uh . . . yeah."

"My name's Jerry Kelly. I'm eleven years old and I used to be a first baseman in Ohio. We just moved here last week. I was watching *Sportsline*. I'd like to try out for The Grandstand team. The one that was on TV just now. We live in Arborville. On Arborview Boulevard."

"That's . . . great. I better write your name and phone number down. Could you hold on?"

I put my hand over the phone.

"It's a kid who wants to be on our team," I shouted.

"Now it starts," Dad said.

I got a pencil and wrote down Jerry Kelly's name and phone number and told him that Mr. Henry or I would call him back.

"He sounds like a great coach," Jerry Kelly said.

"He is," I said.

No sooner did I hang up when the phone rang again. And it was another new kid in town who'd seen *Sportsline* and was eleven years old and wanted to play on The Grandstand team. I took his name and number too.

That was just the beginning. For no sooner did I hang up on his call when the phone rang again. And it was still another kid. And after him, still another. The phone started ringing off the hook. Kid after kid after kid called.

Who would have believed there were that many new eleven-year-old kids in town? And then, wouldn't you know it, I started getting calls from some of the kids we had tried to recruit earlier today and couldn't. Andy van Gasse called. And Victor Perles. And two more kids who'd said they didn't want to play but now had changed their minds. All in all before the phone stopped ringing, I had taken down fifteen names and phone numbers.

"Mom, Dad," I yelled, "we've got a team. A full team and then some."

"From all those calls I think you could start a separate league," Dad said. "Come here and tell us about it."

The phone rang again. Here we go again, I thought.

"Hello."

"Hello," a familiar voice said.

I was so startled I forgot I had been going to call her.

"Kim," I said, "you did it. You really did it. It was you, wasn't it, who called your dad?"

"Yeah."

"I didn't even think of it, I was so scared."

"I was scared too."

"And your dad was so great. He's a genius."

"He's okay. Did you get calls?"

"Are you kidding? As soon as the show ended kids started calling. New kids in town. And some of the kids who turned us down before. Kim, I've got fifteen names, and some of the new kids sound good."

"Did you tell Mr. Henry and Aaron?"

"No."

"You better, Jason. I hope he still wants to coach us."

"Why wouldn't he?"

"Come on, Jason. We heard him say he was Buck McHenry. Maybe he won't want to face us."

She was right. I hadn't even thought of that. And worse, I thought, how was Mr. Henry going to face the Baer Machine kids at Eberwoods School on Monday? And suppose Aaron was ashamed and didn't want to play?

"You still there, Jason?"

"Yeah."

"Are you going to call Mr. Henry and Aaron?"

"Would you do it for me, Kim?"

"Come on, Jason. You're captain. You've also got the names of the new kids. We've got to have a practice tomorrow."

She was right. We had to have a practice tomorrow. We were behind enough as it was. This would be a very hard phone call to make, but I had to grit my teeth and call and find out if Mr. Henry was still willing to coach us and if Aaron was still willing to be on the team.

"Okay, I'll call."

"And call me back," she said.

"Come on in here, Jason," Dad called out.

"I've got one more call to make."

"Who are you going to call now?"

"Mr. Henry. Kim said I had to. She's right."

"Can't you call him tomorrow?" Mom said. "It's getting late."

"It'll be too late tomorrow, Mom. We've got to have a practice tomorrow."

"He better call Mr. Henry," Dad said. "But Jason, make this the last one. Okay?"

"Okay."

The phone rang only once in the Henry house when Mrs. Henry answered it. She must have been sitting on it. Guarding him. People must have been calling them already, I thought dismally.

"Mrs. Henry, it's me. Jason Ross."

Silence. I couldn't tell whether it was a hostile silence or what. Nervously, I filled it.

"Mrs. Henry, did you . . . uh . . . see . . . uh?"

More silence.

"Mrs. Henry, I . . . didn't mean . . . to, uh, make trouble for Mr. Henry."

She hates me, I thought. I don't blame her.

"Who is it this time, Jessie?" I heard Mr. Henry's voice in the background.

"Jason Ross."

Pause. Then, "I want to talk to him."

Now I was in for it. Even his footsteps coming to the phone sounded angry. Kim should have called him. He'd have a harder time being angry at her.

"Jason?"

"Mr. Henry, what I was, uh, calling about is, uh." I stopped. Breathed in. "Did you see the *Sportsline* show, Mr. Henry?" This was awful. I wasn't handling this very well.

"Yes, boy. I saw it. Did you?"

I gulped. "Yes, sir. I thought, uh, it was a, uh, good show."

Silence. "Did you?" I couldn't tell what he was thinking.

Change the subject, I thought. "Mr. Henry, I got fifteen calls from kids who want to play on our team. I got all their names and phone numbers and Kim thinks we should have a practice tomorrow at Sampson Park if it's, uh, okay with you. . . ." My voice died.

More silence. This was it. We either had a coach or we didn't.

"You mean you kids still want me to coach you?"

"Oh, Mr. Henry." My eyes suddenly felt wet again. "Mr. Henry, you're a great coach."

"I'm not Buck McHenry, Jason."

"I'm glad you're not, Mr. Henry."

He laughed. And a load flew off my back on the wings of his laughter. To hear that familiar laugh. It was music.

"Boy, I was telling stories."

"It was my fault, Mr. Henry. I insisted that you were Buck McHenry."

"How did Chuck Axelrod find out, Jason?"

He asked it so fast I wasn't prepared. It was like being fast pitched. I didn't know what to say. I couldn't tell him that Kim and I were trapped below his porch and heard his confession and, worse, heard him cry. This was just terrible.

My silence went on and on. Finally he broke it. "Maybe someday I'll ask the man himself," he said. Then he laughed. "And then again, maybe I won't. It doesn't always pay to inquire too closely into things. Especially when they come out all right in the end. Jason, those kids who called. You tell them to be at Sampson Park tomorrow."

"What time?" I tried to keep the elation out of my voice. I tried to sound matter-of-fact.

"Let's make it one thirty."

"I'll call them right away. How's, uh . . . how's Aaron?"

"He's right here. You want to talk with him?"

"Could I?"

"Aaron, you want to talk with Jason?"

"Yeah," I heard Aaron say.

Mr. Henry said to him, "Jason got fifteen more players for our team."

I didn't hear Aaron's response to that, but a second later he was on the phone.

"Jason," he said.

"How're you doing, man?" I was trying to sound cool.

"Okay. How you doing?"

"Okay." I took a deep breath. "You see the show?"

"Yep. My grampa isn't Buck McHenry."

"I know. It's okay though, isn't it?"

"Wait a second. Grampa, what're you standing round here for?"

I didn't hear what Mr. Henry said. But Aaron then said, "Because I want to talk private with Jason, Grampa. That's why."

Mrs. Henry's voice sounded in the background sharp and clear. "Let them talk privately, Mr. Henry."

Silence. Then I guess Aaron was alone with the phone. "You still there, Jason?"

"Yeah."

"I saw you."

For a moment I didn't understand what he said. He said it so fast.

"What'd you say?"

"We saw you. Me and my grandma."

"What're you talking about, man?"

"Me and my grandma saw you and Kim."

"On TV, you mean?"

I was getting goose bumps. I didn't think he was talking about the TV show at all.

"No. Before then. Grampa heard someone moving around outside the house. He checked the back. Grandma and I checked the front. We saw you and Kim running with your bikes out front."

My knees felt weak. I sat down on a kitchen stool.

"You still there, Jason?"

Barely, I thought. "I'm still here."

"You found out about my grampa then, didn't you?"

"Yes."

"And that's how come Mr. Axelrod found out, isn't it?"

"Yes. Kim called him."

"That's what Grandma and I figured. Grampa doesn't know how he found out."

I said nothing.

"You still there, Jason?"

"Yeah."

"Chuck Axelrod was good on TV, wasn't he?"

A flood of relief came over me. Aaron wasn't

sore. He wasn't sore at me. He wasn't sore at Kim. And most important of all, he didn't sound sore at his grandfather.

"He was great."

"Jason?"

"Yeah."

"My grandma says Grampa made all that stuff up on account of me."

"And me. Aaron?"

"What?"

"I was scared you'd be sore at your grampa."

"Oh, I never believed that stuff anyway."

He wasn't telling the truth. He'd believed just the way I'd believed it, and Kim and her dad and the Baer Machine kids had believed it. We'd all believed. But it was all right. It didn't matter now.

"Did your grampa tell you about the practice tomorrow?" I asked him.

"No."

"Well, we got one. At Sampson Park at one thirty. I've got to say good-bye now. I've got to call fifteen kids. Hey, would you like to call some, Aaron?"

"Sure."

"You could call five kids. I could call five. And Kim could call five. How does that sound?"

"Sounds good. Lemme get a pencil."

And that's what happened. Aaron called five kids. I called up Kim and told her what happened and she agreed to call five kids.

After that I started calling my five kids. I had just started on the first one when Dad came into the kitchen and stared at me. "Jason, you promised."

"Almost all through," I said cheerfully. "Hello, is this Jerry Kelly? Jerry, this is Jason Ross, captain of The Grandstand team. You called me earlier. Well, good news, man, we're going to have a team. Mr. Henry's called a practice for one thirty tomorrow at Sampson Park. Can you make it? Great. Let me tell you how to get there. . . ."

23

We had a great practice the next day. And after that, for game after game after game, we had a great season.

We wound up in third place behind the Bank and Baer Machine. Aaron pitched shutout ball every time out, but the rules are that no kid can pitch more than four innings a game and we didn't have anyone that good after him.

Kim turned out to be one of the best second basemen, excuse me, base persons, in the league. She and Aaron made the all-star team. I didn't. But I got my share of hits and believe it or not some were leg hits, ground balls that I beat out to first. One ground ball I hit against the Bank team I can still hear Mr. Henry shouting, "Hot coals, boy. Hot coals." Reminding me not to look where I hit the ball. Just pick up my feet and run. Which I did. That lesson in the school corridor seemed a long time ago.

Jim Davis wasn't able to get away from the store for any of our games except our first game against Baer Machine. And that was when he met Mr. Henry for the first time.

Jim had a camera around his neck. He stuck out his hand and said to Mr. Henry, "So you're the one Jason insisted was Buck McHenry?"

I almost died. But Mr. Henry chuckled and said, "Not only Jason. I insisted on it too . . . for a while."

Jim thought he was kidding. He laughed. So did Mr. Henry. I sort of smiled weakly.

That game against Baer Machine was the game I worried about most. It wasn't just the game that I worried about. School hadn't yet ended and I worried that the Baer Machine kids had told everyone who went to Eberwoods School about Mr. Henry pretending to be Buck McHenry.

But they hadn't. Aaron told me his grampa said no kid at Eberwoods ever said a thing to him about the Buck McHenry business. Maybe Mr. Borker had something to do with it. He didn't turn out to be such a bad guy after all. Aaron said his grampa told him the kids were respectful to him the rest of the school year.

But would they be respectful in a game situation when it looked like they might lose? Would there be some nasty bench jockeying by them? There wasn't. I think it was mostly because of Aaron's fastball. They knew it wouldn't pay to get Aaron mad. He threw hard enough when he was being friendly. We beat them on their own diamond at Eberwoods, 5–2. They got two runs off Jerry Kelly, who relieved Aaron in the fifth inning. Incidentally, they never called us "bubble gum ballplayers" either, which I was sure they would from the way they used to tease me about my baseball cards. I think they laid off because we were a good team. You never want to rile up a good team.

That game, as I said, was the only one Jim Davis saw, and at that I'm not sure he saw much of it. He spent most of the game taking pictures of everyone. Including Mr. Henry.

Later, we found out why.

About a week after the season ended, Jim gave a team party down at The Grandstand. It was a Sunday afternoon and Jim closed The Grandstand early, which was something since Sunday's his biggest day after Saturday. We had the party in the middle of the main room, smack in the middle of baseball cards, posters, pennants, T-shirts, all the stuff. Jim had ice cream, pizza, pop. Halfway through the party he made a little speech.

"I want to thank all the players who made this such a fantastic season. The Grandstand team didn't exist before the season started and we came in among the top teams. I never had the time to take you kids for pizzas or Dairy Queens. So I'm trying to make up for it now. Also I have a little present for each of you."

Jim then gave each of us a baseball card of ourself. In color. In our Grandstand uniform, batting or running or fielding or throwing. They were made from the pictures he'd taken during the Baer Machine game.

On top of each card our position was listed and so was the name of The Grandstand and its address. Jim's always the businessman.

On the back side, the stats side, it told how we batted and threw and there was inside scoop on each of us.

About me, it said,

JASON ROSS, 11, catcher, bats right, throws right, captain of team, and among those responsible for The Grandstand team being formed.

About Aaron, it said:

AARON HENRY, 11, pitcher, throws right, bats right, voted MVP in Arborville eleven-year-old league, and among those responsible for The Grandstand team being formed. All-Star.

And about Kim, it said:

246

KIM AXELROD, 11, second base, bats right, throws right, tough, feisty ballplayer, good hitter, fastest runner on team, among those responsible for The Grandstand team being formed. All-Star.

Jim also had a card for Mr. Henry. When he gave it to him, there was applause and everyone crowded round to have a look at it. Mr. Henry read it, chuckled, and passed it around.

It was a picture of him coaching during the Baer Machine game. On the stats side it said:

MACK HENRY, former pitcher in semipro leagues in the South, was winning coach in his first year in Arborville eleven-year-old league. Also responsible for The Grandstand team being formed.

It was a swell card, and it linked him and me and Aaron and Kim. Which was as it should be.

Jim also took a lot of kidding about The Grandstand being mentioned so many times. It was a great party.

One Saturday afternoon in the fall Kim and I biked over to Aaron's house with our baseball cards. Mr. Henry was there. Kim's cards were every bit as good as I expected. I brought my best and showed them. My 1955 Mays, my Diamond Stars. Kim showed her incredibly expensive 1952 Mantle. And before you knew it we were back in the discussion about why Mantle's cards were always worth more than Mays's, even for the same years when Mays had the better stats.

I told them what Jim had said about the market determining the price of a card and how it was mostly white kids who collected.

Aaron was very quiet. Mr. Henry, who had been listening, said, "I think Mr. Davis is right. Question is, is he always going to be right?"

I looked up at Mr. Henry. The three of us were seated on the floor. "You mean will more black kids start collecting?"

"I mean more than that, boy. I'm asking if folks'll ever collect baseball cards without noticing what the color of the man's skin on the card is."

None of us had the answer to that.

That evening I repeated Mr. Henry's question to Dad. Would folks ever collect baseball cards without noticing what the color of the man's skin on the card is?

"Jason, I don't have any idea," Dad said.

"Da-ad," I insisted.

Dad looked at me. He was silent for a while, and then he said, "Jason, I think people will only become color-blind about cards when they become color-blind about people."

"When will people become color-blind about people?"

Dad shook his head ruefully. "And I used to think collecting baseball cards was a mindless hobby. Jason, I don't know if people will ever be decent to each other."

"I think someday they will."

"Do you? Well, maybe your generation will have better luck making it happen than ours did."

"We will," I said.

"I hope so," Dad said.

Aaron has started collecting baseball cards. Only his collection is getting smaller instead of getting bigger. He started with two cards besides his own, and now he's down to one.

The first card was the Buck McHenry card—the card that started me off on my search for a legend.

The second card was the card Jim made up for his grampa, Mr. Henry.

So far so good. But then Aaron did a crazy thing. He glued the two cards together on their stats sides so that they made one card. I was shocked.

"What'd you do that for?" I asked him. You're never supposed to fool with baseball cards. You want to keep them in mint condition, if you can.

"They go together, Jason," he said.

"Maybe, but you've ruined the Buck McHenry card. Now you can't trade it or do anything with it."

"I don't want to do anything with it, Jason. I just want to look at it."

And look he did. And I looked with him. What else could you do with that card? We turned it over and over, from young powerful strong Buck McHenry to gray-haired old Mr. Henry back to Buck McHenry again. And after a while that card began to grow on me.

True, it wasn't really a baseball card anymore. It had no value. You couldn't trade it or sell it or do anything with it. All you could do was look at it.

I looked at it, and I remembered that day back in April when I set out to find Buck McHenry and found old Mr. Henry. The day I went looking for a legend and found a man.

"Aaron," I heard myself say, "I'll trade you for that card."

Aaron just laughed.